Mama Tripopulous on How to Hook A Husband

My Demetria, she thinks she knows what the world is about. She works so hard, day and night, to keep the restaurant going. But when it comes to her love life, she has a lot to learn. Back in my day… Oh, well. Lucky for her, Jared Panetta is a persistent young man. I knew the first time he walked in the door that he was the one for my Demi. If only she weren't so stubborn!

But who knows? Maybe a little hard to get is good. Jared seems to be enjoying the challenge. And I can see all the signs—those two are in love up to their elbows! Maybe things are going better than I'd thought. Now where *did* I put that wedding cake recipe…?

Dear Reader,

I remember when I first discovered Greek food. I was in college, and there was a Greek restaurant one door down the street from my apartment. The moment my boyfriend took me there and bought me my first souvlaki, I was in love. Not with him, mind you. (That—foolishly!—came later.) With souvlaki. And moussaka. And pastitsio. Not to mention baklava. I continue to love Greek food to this day, so it's no mystery to me why Jared Panetta, who first encounters Demi Tripopulous when he wants to buy the family restaurant, should not only fall in love with Demi's Greek delicacies but with the woman herself. Soon enough, he's making her *The Offer She Couldn't Refuse.* And for your sake, I hope you don't refuse this newest delight from award-winning author Marie Ferrarella.

Of course, you also shouldn't miss Christie Ridgway's latest: *Ready, Set...Baby!* There's just something about a marriage-of-convenience plot that I can't resist. And luckily for readers everywhere, heroine Katie McKay is equally unable to resist hero Seth Cooper. And it's not just the baby on the way making her feel romantic—it's the man himself. He's a winner—and so is this book.

I hope you enjoy both these wonderful novels, and I also hope you'll come back next month for two more wonderful Yours Truly books all about unexpectedly meeting, dating—and marrying!—Mr. Right.

Yours,

Leslie J. Wainger
Senior Editor and Editorial Coordinator

Please address questions and book requests to:
Silhouette Reader Service
U.S.: 3010 Walden Ave., P.O. Box 1325, Buffalo, NY 14269
Canadian: P.O. Box 609, Fort Erie, Ont. L2A 5X3

MARIE FERRARELLA

The Offer She Couldn't Refuse

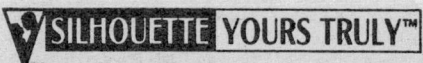

Published by Silhouette Books
America's Publisher of Contemporary Romance

If you purchased this book without a cover you should be aware that this book is stolen property. It was reported as "unsold and destroyed" to the publisher, and neither the author nor the publisher has received any payment for this "stripped book."

To Daddy,
who refused to let me
into his kitchen
(and forced me to learn how
to cook the hard way)

 SILHOUETTE BOOKS

ISBN 0-373-52061-1

THE OFFER SHE COULDN'T REFUSE

Copyright © 1998 by Marie Rydzynski-Ferrarella

All rights reserved. Except for use in any review, the reproduction or utilization of this work in whole or in part in any form by any electronic, mechanical or other means, now known or hereafter invented, including xerography, photocopying and recording, or in any information storage or retrieval system, is forbidden without the written permission of the editorial office, Silhouette Books, 300 East 42nd Street, New York, NY 10017 U.S.A.

All characters in this book have no existence outside the imagination of the author and have no relation whatsoever to anyone bearing the same name or names. They are not even distantly inspired by any individual known or unknown to the author, and all incidents are pure invention.

This edition published by arrangement with Harlequin Books S.A.

® and TM are trademarks of Harlequin Books S.A., used under license. Trademarks indicated with ® are registered in the United States Patent and Trademark Office, the Canadian Trade Marks Office and in other countries.

Printed in U.S.A.

Dearest Reader,

I'll be the first to admit that I have trouble letting go of things. Not as much trouble as my daughter, who, if not for me, would still have every single stuffed animal she'd ever received and every single shred of wrapping paper it came in. But I do like to hang on to things. This could possibly explain why I'm still married to the same man I fell in love with in high school. It also explains why I felt that I had to give Demi her own special romance after introducing her just in passing in *The 7lb., 2oz. Valentine*. I gave a small supporting character (Guy Tripopulous) a warm family, and they in turn needed their own stories. That's the thing about nice people—you want to see them happy. Although the restaurant kept her more than busy, Demi needed someone special to hold and to hold her. But since she lived and breathed work, she wasn't likely to find anyone on her own unless he waltzed into the restaurant, which is just what happened....

If this story gives you a little pleasure, consider it a hug from me to you.

Love,

Marie

Books by Marie Ferrarella

Silhouette Yours Truly
†The 7lb., 2oz. Valentine
Let's Get Mommy Married
Traci on the Spot
Mommy and the Policeman Next Door
**Desperately Seeking Twin...
The Offer She Couldn't Refuse

Silhouette Romance
The Gift #588
Five-Alarm Affair #613
Heart to Heart #632
Mother for Hire #686
Borrowed Baby #730
Her Special Angel #744
The Undoing of Justin Starbuck #766
Man Trouble #815
The Taming of the Teen #839
Father Goose #869
Babies on His Mind #920
The Right Man #932
In Her Own Backyard #947
Her Man Friday #959
Aunt Connie's Wedding #984
‡Caution: Baby Ahead #1007
†Mother on the Wing #1026
‡Baby Times Two #1037
Father in the Making #1078
The Women in Joe Sullivan's Life #1096
†Do You Take This Child? #1145
The Man Who Would Be Daddy #1175
Your Baby or Mine? #1216
**The Baby Came C.O.D. #1264

Silhouette Special Edition
It Happened One Night #597
A Girl's Best Friend #652
Blessing in Disguise #675
Someone To Talk To #703
World's Greatest Dad #767
Family Matters #832
She Got Her Man #843
Baby in the Middle #892
Husband: Some Assembly Required #931
Brooding Angel #963
†Baby's First Christmas #997
Christmas Bride #1069
Wanted: Husband, Will Train #1132

Silhouette Desire
†Husband: Optional #988

Silhouette Intimate Moments
*Holding Out for a Hero #496
*Heroes Great and Small #501
*Christmas Every Day #538
Callaghan's Way #601
*Caitlin's Guardian Angel #661
†Happy New Year—Baby! #686
The Amnesiac Bride #787
Serena McKee's Back in Town #808

Fortune's Children
Forgotten Honeymoon

Silhouette Books
Silhouette Christmas Stories 1992
"The Night Santa Claus Returned"

‡Baby's Choice
†The Baby of the Month Club
*Those Sinclairs
**Two Halves of a Whole

Books by Marie Ferrarella writing as Marie Nicole

Silhouette Desire
Tried and True #112
Buyer Beware #142
Through Laughter and Tears #161
Grand Theft: Heart #182
A Woman of Integrity #197
Country Blue #224
Last Year's Hunk #274
Foxy Lady #315
Chocolate Dreams #346
No Laughing Matter #382

Silhouette Romance
Man Undercover #373
Please Stand By #394
Mine by Write #411
Getting Physical #440

1

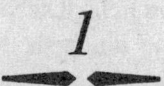

"...And in conclusion, I am sure we can arrive at an amount that will prove to be mutually satisfactory to all parties involved."

"Mutually satisfactory, my foot." Why was she even bothering to waste her time reading this condescending garbage through to the end?

Angry with herself and the sender, Demetria Tripopulous balled up the letter between her hands and tossed it toward the wastepaper basket in her small office. Even at close range, the uneven ball skimmed against the rim and then landed on the floor beside the basket.

"You missed."

Startled, she whirled around in the swivel chair that, along with the desk, basket and file cabinet, took up all the available space within the windowless office. She didn't have to look to know who it was. Guy, making one of his pit stops. Normally, though she made a point not to admit it, she welcomed the sight of her older brother. But today she wasn't feeling particularly friendly.

With a careless shrug, Demi rose to her feet. "Some of us didn't have time to shoot baskets after school when we were in high school." Picking up the letter, she threw it in the trash. "Some of us had a sense of responsibility and went to help out where we were needed."

The jab was unfair and she knew it. It was choice more than duty that had had her putting in more hours at the family restaurant than Guy. He'd been an all-around athlete who'd had legitimate demands on his time. And he'd had dreams that took him beyond the kitchen and the tables out front.

Her dreams were all bound up here.

To each his own, she supposed.

"Aw, give it a rest, Demi."

Sergeant Augustus "Guy" Tripopulous's mouth curved in tolerant affection as he leaned a shoulder against the doorjamb of the tiny room that was no bigger than a large cubicle. From within this room, his grandfather, then his father, had run the family restaurant. Now the ball had appropriately been passed to Demi, bypassing Guy to his eternal, undying relief. Demi was a lot better at this sort of thing than he was. But it had taken the combined persuasive powers of both of them and Theo, their grandfather, to convince their father that there was no shame in letting a female member of the family take over and run the restaurant. So far, Demi had done a better job than either one of her predecessors.

She was upset, he thought, recognizing the signs, and wondered what was up. He knew better than to ask. Demi didn't like being—as she called it—"interrogated." She either volunteered the information on her own or remained silent on the subject. He wasn't about to get his head bitten off.

The more easygoing of the two, Guy drawled, "You know, you've been playing that old tune so long, it's ready to collect Social Security."

She pushed past him into the kitchen, her mind still on the letter. Who the hell did this Winfield character think he was, trying to buy her out?

Demi didn't spare Guy a glance as she crossed to the large oven, but she knew her brother had followed her. She also knew without looking that the baklava was ready. Walnut this time. She nodded to her cousin George, silently reminding him to take the pastry out.

"So, did you stop by to harass me?" She debated putting on a fresh apron and decided against it. Lena would be back soon. She glanced toward the rear door leading to the alleyway. Hopefully. "Slow day on the streets, Sergeant Tripopulous?" A smile rose to her lips as George took out the baklava. Perfect. Every one of them.

"I stopped by to get one of these." With fingers accustomed to skimming things off a hot baking sheet, Guy plucked a prize up for himself, then passed it back and forth between his cupped hands until it cooled sufficiently for him to pop it into his mouth. He'd had a weakness for baklava ever since he was a small boy, and Demi made the best around. "And a little friendly conversation."

Demi shook her head. How could he bear to eat something so hot? The man had a mouth made out of asbestos. Still, she liked watching his reaction. It was as close as he came to giving her a compliment. She'd taken a treasured family recipe and improved on it, adding her own special twist. The result was, to quote one of her friends, "a bit of heaven that was to die for."

Guy closed his eyes, savoring the taste as it melted into his tongue and slid down his throat. He sighed, content, then opened his eyes again.

"Good thing the food's sweeter than you are." He dusted off his hands as he followed her through the swinging door out into the dining area. "I have a few things I need to ask Theo. He around?"

The question was rhetorical. Demi wondered why he even bothered asking. Their grandfather was where he had been every afternoon for the last fifteen years.

"Back booth, frowning over his next move." She didn't bother pointing. Guy knew the way blindfolded and spun around like a top. They'd both grown up here. Every memory worth having was tied up somehow to this small square footage.

Demi could do with a little of that laid-back attitude that Theo had adopted, Guy mused. The old man would probably outlive them all, he thought fondly. Debating, he stole a tiny mint chocolate wrapped in green foil from beside the register. These, too, were made on the premises. "Game progress any?"

Demi laughed shortly. "No one's made a move in so long, the pieces are collecting dust." This time she did gesture toward the rear of the restaurant. Her grandfather and one of the restaurant's oldest customers, his best friend, Alex, sat in the last booth, embroiled in a chess game as if the fate of the world depended on the outcome. "Look at them. They look like they're posing for a still life."

She could remember her grandfather moving around the kitchen like a short, squat bull, ordering his wife, daughter-in-law and sister around like a dictator who hadn't quite decided whether or not he wanted to be thought of as benevolent. He'd had the place running like clockwork. There'd always seemed to be people everywhere back then. Sometimes they'd had to turn patrons away because there hadn't been enough room to seat them all. She missed those days, Demi thought. Missed just being able to watch and know that everything was all right because someone else was taking care of it.

Now it was she who had to take care of everything, to keep everything moving along through good times and bad. There were times...

The hell with waiting for Demi to tell him what was eating her. Guy got into his sister's face, hoping to catch her off guard. "You're even testier than usual, Demi. Anything wrong?"

It was on the tip of her tongue to snap at him, to say that he had picked a fine time to get interested in the business. But he wasn't interested in the business—he was interested in her, and she knew it. Chagrined at her reaction, she banked it down and shrugged, then wove her fingers through the black hair that rioted around her face like a dark storm.

"The rats are creeping out of the woodpile."

They had neither a woodpile nor rats, but pointing that out would only irritate her further. Guy knew the value of silence in his line of work. The suspect usually talked if given enough of an opportunity to unburden himself.

His question had made her think of the letter, and Demi became angry all over again. The gall, the unmitigated gall of them, to think that she'd sell something that had her family's sweat and tears in it. "It seems we've caught the eye of Winfield, Inc."

Guy folded his arms in front of him and gave her his undivided attention. "The restaurant chain?" Why would the fast-growing local organization contact them? Her restaurant certainly wasn't doing enough business lately to merit attention. Demi didn't talk about it, but every time he had dropped by in the last couple of months, about half the booths and tables were empty. Of course, they'd had slumps before and always managed to come back stronger than ever. Maybe that was what Winfield had in mind.

Demi barely nodded. She didn't like this feeling; it was as if she were suddenly under siege. It was bad enough that the bills were mounting up. "It seems they want us to become 'part of the family.'"

Their late father had been quite vocal about what he thought of the organization that was bent on building a restaurant monopoly in the county. The tirade had been long and wordy, and none of it pleasant. He'd been gone for over a year now, but the sentiment still held.

"Family of what, sharks?" Guy asked.

The furrow in the middle of her brow softened as she looked at her brother. He was older, but she'd always felt responsible for him. That was part of her problem, she supposed. She felt responsible for everyone. "Nice to know we agree on some things."

"Did they quote a price?"

One of the bulbs along the wall was out, she noticed. She had to see about getting that replaced before they were officially serving dinner. Romantic was one thing, dim was another.

Absently Demi shook her head. "No, they said something about negotiating and arriving at a settlement 'mutually satisfactory' to both of us." Demi looked at him sharply as the question solidified in her mind. "Why? Would you be interested if they had?"

He knew that tone. If it had belonged to a marksman, it would have come a moment before a rifle was discharged at a target. "Just curious."

"Well, stuff it," she told him tersely. "Nobody's getting this place."

It'd been a hard morning for him, following on the heels of a hard night. The twins both had bad colds, which meant that neither he nor Nancy had gotten a lot of sleep. He'd come in to face a mound of paperwork he'd been putting off. He wasn't at his best right now and Demi's mood wasn't helping.

Guy looked around. The restaurant could do with a coat of paint and a couple of the booths needed to be reupholstered. Not to mention that the mural depicting the Olympic Games could stand to be touched up and refreshed. He thought of the outstanding tabs on accounts that were kept open, accounts belonging to people his father had carried from time to time, and his father before him. Extending credit to people down on their luck was almost a family tradition. And though Demi would rather die than admit it, business *was* down of late, and it was taking its toll on her.

He was thinking more of her than the restaurant when he said, "Yeah, real slice of heaven, this place."

He didn't love the restaurant the way she did. Guy had always gone his own way. She was the one with one foot in the past, one in the present. She was the one who loved this old place for what it was and what it had been as well as for what it could be. She didn't fault Guy for the way he felt, but right now she was a little less than tolerant.

Because there were only the old-timers around to

bear witness to what she did, Demi whacked her brother upside his head with the heel of her hand the way she used to do when they were kids. "Yes, it's a slice of heaven, and don't you forget it."

Guy swallowed a groan. "You've got to do something about that winsome way of yours," he told her, rubbing his head. The man who finally wound up with his sister was going to have to have a hard head if he hoped to survive, Guy thought.

Theodore Tripopulous squinted, barely making out the forms of his grandchildren. He didn't have to see. Their outlines were as familiar to him as the palms of his own hands. A voice made smooth by years of anisette warned, "Demetria, Augustus, not in front of the customers."

Demi glanced toward the last booth, her chin lifted in defiance. "What customers? There's only family."

Theo shook his snow-white head and sighed as he looked at Alex across the chess board. "Fifty years younger than me and I am the one with the good vision."

Then, to emphasize his point, he removed the pipe that was as much a part of him as his mouth was and pointed with the tip toward the entrance. He looked back down at the board, dismissing everything else but the move that he had yet to make.

Demi turned and saw a well-dressed, dark-haired man standing just within the entrance. Oh, great, and here she was, behaving like a shrew. Slanting an annoyed look at Guy for forcing her to hit him and embarrass herself, Demi squared her small shoulders.

Instantly, right before his eyes, the girl she'd been was gone, transforming into the hostess of Aphrodite, a family-styled restaurant that prided itself on its fine, old-world Greek cuisine. It was a little like watching a magic act, Guy mused.

She didn't care to be his source of amusement. "Don't you have someone to arrest or something?" she whispered as she passed her brother.

He grinned. "I'll be on my way as soon as I talk to Theo. You go do your thing." Turning his back on her, Guy made his way to his grandfather's booth. The scent of anisette and cherry wood guided him.

Her thing. Leave it to Guy to trivialize the maintenance of a family tradition, making it sound like nothing more than mundane habit. She dearly loved him, but there were times she wanted to double up her fists and pummel him.

Like now.

Her mood wasn't his fault, she reminded herself. It was the fault of that letter. She'd only just now had the opportunity to read it, even though, by its postmark, it had arrived over two weeks ago. Quarterly tax time had come breathing down her neck and she'd let everything else slide while she went over the books. Demi still did the books herself. The idea of letting someone else do it was tempting, but that would mean paying someone else and right now that was out of the question.

She should have buried the damn letter instead of reading it.

Why was she letting it get to her? Just because Winfield, Inc., was an organization that was slowly eating up some of the other independent restaurants in the area didn't mean they were going to do the same with hers. It was just that...

Just that she was afraid, she thought. Afraid of messing up, of losing the business. Of losing something that meant so much to her family.

Enough. There was a paying customer to seat and a hundred things that needed her attention. She'd wasted enough time on the letter, its implication and the sharks who had sent it.

"Hello. Welcome to Aphrodite." With an easy sweep of her hand, she picked up the dark green menu from the hostess desk, her fingers brushing along the raised gold letters. "I'm your hostess. Do you have any preferences as to seating?" She smiled at the man and inclined her head toward the interior of the restaurant. "As you can see, you're in luck. You can have your choice of several very nice locations."

The woman had a voice like dark whiskey subtly poured over ice in a very tall glass. It went right through a man, straight to his gut. Jared Panetta returned the smile he found beguiling.

"Anyplace is fine."

"Ah, an easy man." Her eyes bid him welcome, as did the gentle sway of her hips as she turned to lead him to a table. "My mother always said to beware of an easy man."

Rather than walk behind her and enjoy the view, Jared stayed abreast. He regarded her profile and calculated just how long it would take him to make her come around. "Oh, and why is that?"

"They get you off your guard." Stopping at a table that was centrally located, Demi set the menu down in front of a place setting. "Here you are—our finest table." She gestured around for his benefit. "A view of the entire restaurant."

He slid into the chair. The only view that looked interesting from where he sat was standing right in front of him. But he was here on business, so he surveyed the area, taking in its atmosphere.

It could do with some work, he decided. But all in all, it would be a fine addition to the chain.

Jared raised his eyes to the woman before him. "So I see." A loud exclamation from the rear drew his attention. "What's going on back there?"

One of the men had finally made a move. From the sound of it, the move had belonged to Theo. Alex was not happy about it. Her mouth curved fondly. Alex hated losing. "Oh, that's just Theo and Alex."

Jared leaned forward to get a better view. "It looks like...they're playing chess?" He looked at her questioningly.

She laughed at the confused expression on his face. But the sound was so friendly, he couldn't find himself taking offense.

"'Playing' is a generous way to put it. Actually, a more accurate description would be to say that they're staring at chess pieces. You just happened in when one of them made a move." There was pleasure in her eyes as she regarded the two. "This is tantamount to an historic moment."

He still didn't understand. "But I thought this was a restaurant."

Because she was so accustomed to having the chess game in progress, Demi didn't immediately see the reason for his confusion. "It is."

Jared opened the menu and perused both sides. "Chess pieces on the menu?"

Demi glanced around. The other handful of customers were all regulars, all given to lingering over their coffee or, in Mr. Savalas's case, his anisette. There was no hurry and no other customer for her to tend to. So, because the customer asked, she gave him an abbreviated history of the restaurant.

"For them," she acknowledged. "Theo's my grandfather. He started Aphrodite. In the afternoon, when business was slow, he and Alex would play a little chess. Just because he retired didn't mean he had to give up his pleasures. Theo is very big on tradition." She'd always admired that about him. To her, it was the glue that kept things together when times were rough. "So am I," she added after a beat.

Jared set down the menu and leaned back in his chair, going over the information that had been given to him as he studied her face. The photograph he'd been supplied with must have been taken by an imbecile who didn't know his way around a camera. The photograph didn't begin to do her justice. "Then you're the owner?"

As if anyone could actually own a tradition. She extended her hand to him. "Demetria Tripopulous, at your service. But I'm not really the owner."

His hand holding hers, Jared stared at her. He seriously doubted he'd been misinformed. "I don't understand."

She smiled, pride getting the better of her. "The restaurant owns me. I'm more of the keeper of the flame, so to speak." Like an Olympic torch, overseeing the restaurant had been passed to her. But the imprint of other hands on the torch was ever-present.

But he didn't want to hear about that, she thought. Demi nodded at the menu, getting back to business. "So, what will it be?"

"You're the waitress, too?" The report on his desk said that business had fallen off a little of late. Had that been an understatement? Just how bad *was* business when a third-generation owner had to double as a hostess *and* waitress?

Since her father had first tied an apron around her middle when she was ten, Demi had worked every position there was within Aphrodite, including scrubwoman. Her early training came in handy.

"Today, I'm almost everything. One of the waitresses called in sick, the other is on her break." And taking much too long, she thought. But then, she was almost positive she'd seen Lena's fiancé sneak in around back just as she was going out. Another ten minutes wouldn't kill her. After that, she would go out to get Lena. "It's slow this time of day."

There was no resentment in her voice at having to wait tables. He found that interesting. "Are you also the cook?"

The question was asked so engagingly, Demi forgot that she was coaxing his order out of him.

"On occasion. Other times, Theo does the honors." Of all of them, he was the best, she thought. It was his compliments she strove for and held dearest when they finally came. "He likes to keep his hand in. Then there's my mother, my grandmother and my cousin George. He's the one we pay to do it."

Demi abruptly stopped, studying the man. Though she was friendly, she didn't usually spend this much time talking to a customer, especially not before an order was placed. There was a certain rhythm she liked to follow with her customers, a rhythm that had been temporarily lost amid his questions. Despite his gregarious manner, there was an edgy air about him, like someone who had just recently stopped running in order to catch his breath before he resumed a race.

She indicated the menu with her eyes. "You ask a lot of questions for a man who hasn't ordered yet."

To oblige her, he opened the menu again. His tastes ran to meat and potatoes, which was ironic, given his line of work. "What's good today?"

"Everything."

He looked up at her dubiously. "Really?"

She gave him an honest answer. "If it wasn't, it wouldn't be on the menu."

He sincerely doubted that. Every restaurant he'd ever had anything to do with always had hits and misses. It was only natural.

"Well," he admitted, allowing her the lie, "I'm not really very hungry." He hadn't come to eat, but rather to look the place over and observe. Setting the menu down, he folded his hands and looked at Demi. "How about some coffee and dessert?"

If he wasn't hungry, what was he doing in the restaurant to begin with? He wasn't like the regulars, who came to talk and nibble, or, in Alex's case, to play chess and reminisce. Unlike other customers, the regulars came rain or shine, because this was their home away from home. They were people she'd come to know and, in some cases, love as she was growing up above the restaurant. People her grandparents and then her parents counted among their friends. It was no secret that during the years after the Second World War, when times were difficult, Theodore Tripopulous could always be counted on to feed your pinched belly and give you a hot cup of coffee that not only put you back on your feet but had you moving quickly, as well.

It was the sort of reputation Demi took pride in. He was the kind of man she was proud to be directly related to.

That was why disappointing him was something

she lived in fear of. The restaurant represented his life's accomplishments.

Demi regarded the man at the table, wondering what had prompted him to come. "What kind of dessert would you like?"

Jared left the selection up to her. "Why don't you surprise me?"

Surprises—the man wanted surprises. She walked away, bemused and shaking her head.

Demi returned almost immediately, a demitasse cup of coffee in one hand, and in the other, a plate with the same baklava that her brother had driven three miles out of his way to get. She set both down in front of the customer, then stood back and waited for him to take his first taste.

Jared eyed the delicate china cup. Tiny pink roses were painted on it and along the rim of the saucer. Hand painted, if he wasn't mistaken. There was a certain charm to it, he allowed. But charm only went so far, and he was thinking profit. He knew that the restaurant had an excellent reputation. He'd come to see if it was merited.

"Kind of a small cup, isn't it?" His hand felt almost clumsy as he picked it up.

She could tell what he was thinking: there wasn't enough. The cup held only half the amount found in a regular one. "It's not the size, but the taste," Demi assured him.

He put it to the test, taking a sip that all but depleted the contents. Jared's eyes were watering by the time he set the cup down again. He reached for the water glass. The water did little to cut the thickness of the liquid he'd swallowed.

Jared looked down at the cup. "What's in that?"

She couldn't suppress her grin. "Initially, espresso. The rest is a family secret."

After a moment, when the first impression had time to settle, Jared found himself thinking that the taste was unique. Definitely one that could be acquired.

He wondered if that was true of everything here. Jared eyed the baklava. "Should I be braced?"

She glanced back and saw that her brother was still here and watching the customer with amusement. "Only for extreme pleasure. Go ahead." She gestured toward the plate. "No one's complained yet."

That might be because their throats were paralyzed by the coffee, Jared thought, gamely biting into the cylindrical tube. Tiny golden crumbs as light as snowflakes drizzled down from his lips as they closed over the pastry.

He raised an eyebrow in obvious appreciation. "And this is—?"

Baklava was nothing new. But the way she prepared it, right down to the almost translucent phyllo wrapped around the confection, was. "Also a family secret."

Though he was tempted to finish the dessert in another bite, Jared set it down on the plate. Enjoying a new taste sensation was not why he had been sent here.

"Ms. Tripopulous," Jared sighed, reaching into his pocket, "I'd like to make you an offer I feel you won't be able to refuse." He placed on the table a copy of the letter the corporation had sent her two weeks ago.

The satisfied smile faded from Demi's lips.

2

"You're with Winfield?"

So, she had read the letter, Jared thought. He didn't miss the steely tone that had entered her voice, nor the very solemn look that had taken over her exotic features. She was probably preparing to play cagey. He was up for that. It was the nature of the game. Jared inclined his head.

"Yes."

Demi said nothing. Her only response was to dramatically remove from his table the plate with the half-eaten dessert. Taking it, she turned on her heel and walked away.

Jared had no way of knowing that she was too angry to speak, but the others in the restaurant did. They settled in to watch the fireworks.

He sat there a moment, a little stunned at her abruptness, before leaping to his feet. Skirting around an amused patron who inconveniently chose that time to rise and get in his way, Jared was quick to catch up to Demi before she made it into the kitchen. Rather than follow, he moved to block her path.

"Wait a minute, we need to talk."

Since he was standing directly in front of her, she stopped. For the moment. "No, we don't. *You* need to leave."

Interpreting her body language, Jared automatically took hold of her wrist to keep her from disappearing behind the swinging door.

"You don't understand, Ms. Tripopulous. I'm prepared to give you a very lucrative offer."

Jack Winfield had authorized upping the ante if Jared felt the owner was going to be stubborn about the sale. In Jared's studied opinion, it was definitely shaping up that way.

Winfield wanted this restaurant, with its unique reputation and its distinctive cuisine, under his expanding umbrella of restaurants. Rather than a single theme, he was after quality and variety. Whatever the appetite, there was a Winfield restaurant to fit the bill, ready and willing to serve. By the end of the decade, Winfield was determined to make his name synonymous with dining out in Orange County.

Demi stood stone still, the fire in her eyes so hot, Jared was surprised he didn't just burst into flame where he stood.

Definitely stubborn, he decided.

The quiet hum of voices in the room that she was accustomed to had ceased. Except for the soft, piped-in music, the restaurant had fallen completely silent. Everyone's attention was focused on the scene taking place in front of the kitchen door.

She was barely aware of the others. Only of the annoying man blocking her way.

"No, *you* don't understand, Mr. Making-you-an-offer-you-can't-refuse. The answer is no—a resounding, firm, unequivocal *no*." She glared at the fingers wrapped around her wrist. "And, if you're not prepared to lose that hand, I suggest you take it off my wrist. Now."

His hand went up immediately, not in surrender but in acquiescence. Gauging her response, he regrouped. Winfield hadn't sent him just to feel her out. He had a specific agenda. Jared was good at what he did and what he did now was to dig in.

Mildly aware of the stares he was garnering, he pursued Demi and the matter at hand. "You haven't even heard the offer."

She gritted her teeth. The imbecile in the expensive, well-cut suit knew his employer had sent a letter. "I've read the offer."

"This is a new one. A...shall I say, more generous one." He watched her face, waiting for the storm clouds to shift.

Typical. He thought it was about money, she thought contemptuously. People who worked for corporations that bought out people's dreams always thought it was about money.

"I don't want to hear that offer," Demi ground out evenly.

There were too many witnesses around for her to hit him, although she sorely wished she could. Who the hell did he think he was, coming here and presuming that he could just toss her a sum of money in exchange for what she'd worked for, what her family had worked for, all these years?

"Why?" His voice, silky, had just a touch of seduction about it. Demi found it annoyingly unnerving. He racked up another strike against him. "Afraid it might tempt you to sell?"

Which was exactly what he knew it would do. Extrapolated, it was the kind of offer that might tempt the pope to sell the Vatican.

The new expression on her face was not the one he'd anticipated. The woman looked furious. He had never seen anger look quite as formidable. Or as appealing. Though it had absolutely no effect on the reason he was here, Jared suddenly realized what the clichéd phrase concerning a woman looking magnificent when she was angry actually meant. Because Demetria Tripopulous looked magnificent. Her cheeks took on a flush and her eyes blazed with a hypnotic green fire. Even her hair seemed to swirl about her face like black, brooding storm clouds.

Everything about her was alive and vital. And damn captivating.

Because people were listening, she didn't curse his soul and his damned offer to the lowest depths of hell. But she thought about it.

As she wet her lips to cut the dryness, her eyes fired twin bolts aimed at his arrogance. "You couldn't possibly offer me enough money to tempt me, mister—what the hell is your name, anyway?"

He met her ire with calm, which provoked her even more. "Panetta. Jared Panetta." As quick and as smoothly as a magician, Jared reached into his pocket to produce his business card and held it out to her. "My pager number's on the card. You can reach me anytime."

Seeming to oblige him, Demi put out her hand. But just as the card touched her fingertips, she smugly withdrew it. The card fell to the floor, silently telling him what she thought of him, his card and his company.

"I won't be needing your name, your pager number or your card," she told him flatly. Her mouth hardened into the most tempting line he'd ever seen. Jared had never felt so stirred by a challenge. "Or you."

The look in his eyes said "Want to bet?" as plainly as if he'd said the words out loud. Demi had the momentarily unsettling feeling that he was serving her notice. On more than one level. Demi squared her shoulders, as if to shrug the feeling off.

Not about to be plowed under, Jared rose to the obvious challenge. He left the card lying on the floor. To scramble in front of her and pick it up would be a tactical error, a sign of weakness.

Besides, if he left it there, she could pick it up later. He was betting she would. No one walked away from the kind of money that was sitting on the table, no matter how gorgeous they appeared when breathing fire.

"I'd consider that statement very carefully if I were you."

She was so angry, she realized that she was almost shaking. With almost superhuman control, she composed herself. He'd probably think she was trembling because she was succumbing to him. That was undoubtedly how he ran his deals when it came to women. Oiling them to death with his charm and his looks. Well, he'd just met his Waterloo.

"There is nothing to consider, Mr. Panetta. Aphrodite is not for sale. Not today, not tomorrow and not at any price." And that, she thought, should be that.

She made it sound as if she was talking about the goddess rather than a small restaurant that Winfield's researcher said was bogged down in a temporary cash-flow problem. You'd think she would jump at the chance to get out, save her skin and make some money while she was at it. Obviously the woman didn't have the brains she was born with. But, he thought almost involuntarily, she certainly seemed to have improved on everything else she was born with.

He noticed that it was getting rather warm in the restaurant.

Jared refocused on her words, and not the way her breasts rose and fell as she delivered them. "Ms. Tripopulous, everything has a price."

"*That* is your first mistake." The fire in her eyes

temporarily left, giving way to frost. She looked at him coolly, her eyes passing over him as if he were nothing more than an insignificant insect she was debating whether or not to waste her energy and time squashing. Never mind that he was a handsome insect who seemed to disturb her almost more than the situation warranted. "I'm sure it won't be your last, but it'll be the last mistake you'll commit here." With that, she made her exit.

No retort came to his lips. He watched in silence as the kitchen door swung shut in his face.

Unwilling to make the long walk to the front door with several sets of eyes watching him—and, more importantly, completely unwilling to be so cavalierly dismissed by a woman who barely came up to his shoulder—Jared pushed open the swinging door and followed her into the kitchen.

Demi threw the plate with Jared's half-consumed dessert on the nearest counter and swung around when she heard him enter. Couldn't this guy take a hint?

Hands on her hips, she barred his way any farther into the area. From the corner of her eye, she saw her cousin look up in surprise. "Nobody's allowed back here except employees, Mr. Panetta."

"So hire me," he retorted.

Jared pulled up abruptly as his words echoed in his head. She was making him lose his composure. That had never happened before. Nobody ever got beneath his skin like that. Mentally, he took hold of himself. He wasn't going to accomplish anything by relating to her on a personal level. She wasn't a woman, she was an owner, someone to be cajoled, to be convinced. Any other thoughts floating through his head were superfluous and only got in the way.

He banked them down.

Demi's eyes narrowed. "My brother's a cop," she warned.

His easy manner once more in place, Jared shrugged. "Mine's an assistant D.A. We should have a party sometime and have them meet."

She lifted her chin. If he didn't know better, he would have said there was a look of smug triumph on her face. "Maybe someday, but you can meet mine now." She gestured toward the door he'd just used. "He's standing right behind you."

Guy stepped forward as Jared turned to look. Demi thought of a lone sheriff loping his way across Main Street in a grade B Western. Guy would have probably liked that image.

Guy raised an eyebrow. "Trouble, Demi?"

The smug look on her face deepened as she kept her eyes on Jared. "I don't think so. Mr. Panetta was just leaving. Weren't you, Mr. Panetta?"

He had no intentions of going anywhere. "Jared," he corrected.

In his experience, people had more trouble saying no when they were on a first-name basis with a person. He flashed an easy smile at Guy. Maybe her brother had some influence over her. It was worth a shot. Besides, he made it a point to try to get along with people whenever possible. Life was easier that way.

Jared put out his hand. "I'm with Winfield, Inc."

Guy shook his hand because, Demi's opinion not withstanding, there was no reason to be rude. Yet.

"So I gathered." Guy nodded toward the dining room and the scene that had just played itself out on the other side of the door. "I also gathered that Demi told you she wasn't interested in your company's offer."

Jared was amicable, but firm. He'd been sent to negotiate and that was what he had yet to do. "How could she not be interested in something she hasn't heard yet? The offer I have in my pocket supersedes the one she received in the letter."

The smile on Guy's lips was full of pity. Who better than he knew that Jared was hitting his head against a stone wall?

"Demi makes her mind up quickly. And then you'd have more luck single-handedly moving Mount Rushmore to Brooklyn than changing her mind once it's made up. Demi's a very stubborn woman."

She'd had just about enough of this conversation. Demi glared at both men. "Demi is also very much alive and shouldn't be talked about as if she were dead or in some other room."

Yes, she certainly was very much alive, Jared thought, as appreciation for what he saw once more sneaked into his consciousness.

Shifting gears, he looked into her eyes. The thought

that he should anchor himself to something to keep from falling in crossed his mind. Her eyes looked bottomless. As did her ire.

"My point exactly. So, if you'll just give me a few moments so that I can talk to you, I'm sure you'll see that—"

Demi shook her head and turned away from him. This had gone on long enough. She had a restaurant to run and an inventory waiting to be done. "Sorry, can't spare it. I'm very busy."

He could be just as tenacious as she was. "Ms. Tripopulous—"

With the same effortless movements that made him a good cop and quick on his feet, Guy placed himself between his sister and the man from the restaurant chain. There was no malice behind his smile, just quiet authority. "She said she's busy."

Demi's head jerked up. There he went, playing the big brother role to the hilt. Did Guy think she was helpless? With a sweep of her hand, she pushed him aside. "I can handle my own battles, thank you."

The next moment, the sound of the rear door opening and then closing again caught Demi's attention. She hoped it was Lena, back from her break, and not who she was afraid it was.

One glance over her shoulder told her the woman striding forward was not Lena.

Sharp, pale green eyes quickly assessed the situation and parties involved. A smile lifted the corners of a mouth that was quick to soothe, quick to counsel.

Her eyes on the stranger, Antoinette Tripopulous pushed up the sleeves of her sweater. "Demetria, who is this man?"

Demi and Guy's mother took careful measure of the stranger in their midst. Liking what she saw, she swiftly tailored the man to the exact fit of a potential future son-in-law.

Demi suppressed a groan. She knew that look in her mother's eyes. It was there every time Antoinette saw a living, breathing male over the age of consent. Of the old school way of thinking, her mother didn't think a woman was whole until she was part of a man. No amount of arguing could sway her from that antiquated position.

Demi moved closer to Guy. "With her, I need help," she whispered.

The look he gave her said he'd think about it. Frowning, Demi went through the motions of a half-hearted introduction.

"This is Mr. Panetta, Ma." She gestured at him carelessly, as if he wasn't worth the effort it took to speak. "He was just on his way out." Demi looked at him pointedly. Eventually, he was going to have to take the blatant hint. "Weren't you, Mr. Panetta?"

"So soon?" Antoinette asked, disappointed.

Any ally in a storm, Jared thought as he smiled broadly at the older woman. He moved to Antoinette's side, taking her hand in his and shaking it warmly. "Actually, I can spare a few more minutes."

"Wonderful." As if they were old friends, Antoinette slipped her arm through his. Making people feel at home had been second nature to her for over thirty years. "You will have to excuse Demetria. She gets a little testy after working so hard." Antoinette shook her head sadly. "It is only eleven and she has already put in a full day's work."

She inclined her head toward him as if to share a confidence. Jared noted that there was hardly any gray in her hair. Maybe she didn't spend all that much time with her daughter.

"Do you know that she's been working at the restaurant since she was a little girl? Oh, not full-time, of course, but every moment she could spare, she was here, helping. Learning." Antoinette beamed at her daughter, the source of both her pride and her despair. "A woman could not ask for a better daughter. And she cooks—" Rather than describe any particular dish, she kissed her fingers, then sprang them apart, as if she was releasing a font of exquisite tastes upon the world.

Usually, this kind of thing was just embarrassing. This time Demi added annoying to the tally. Trying to hold on to her temper, she said very evenly, "Ma, you don't have to try to sell me to him."

Antoinette looked shocked at the accusation. "Ah, I am not selling, Demetria, I am extolling your good points." Eyes that saw far beneath the surface of things looked at Demi pointedly. "They sometimes get lost when you open your mouth."

Helpless with frustration, Demi turned to her brother. "Guy?"

He figured he had let her twist in the wind long enough. "Ma." Guy carefully extricated his mother's arm from Jared's. "Theo said he wanted to see you."

Antoinette cringed in resignation at her father-in-law's name. "What does that old man want now?" With a shake of her head, she preceded Guy out the door.

"I owe you," Demi whispered to him as he began to follow his mother out.

Guy grinned at her. "And don't think I won't collect."

Antoinette glanced over her shoulder before she disappeared into the dining room. "Don't leave, Mr. Panetta, I will be right back."

Mercifully for Demi, the door swung shut. Then it was just her, the loathsome stranger and George. George didn't count.

Jared smiled at the closed door. "She's quite a lady."

In a way, Mrs. Tripopulous reminded him of his own mother. There was that same warmth. He'd mistakenly believed that all women were born with it to a greater or lesser degree. It had taken Gloria to show him how deluded he'd been.

The next moment, he was surprised when instead of commenting, Demi took hold of his arm and began leading him away from the door. "Are we going somewhere?"

"We aren't, but you are." She was prepared to drag him if she had to, but he came willingly enough, an amused expression on his face she found particularly annoying. She had no doubt that he used his looks to his advantage. And to her disadvantage if she let him. "Out the back way. Before my mother gets back and posts our banns."

He would have found that amusing if it didn't seem as if it contained more than a kernel of truth in it. Still, he did have a goal to accomplish. "But we haven't talked yet."

She didn't stop until she was at the rear entrance. Still holding on to his arm in case he had any thoughts about doubling back, she replied, "Yes, we have. And if you can't remember the gist of our conversation, I can sum it up for you in one word." Demi pursed her lips together. "No. If you want the long version, just play the word over and over again in your head. Eventually, you'll get the idea."

He'd been told no by people before and always managed to break them down. This was just going to be a little trickier.

"You could retire a rich woman. Do what you've always wanted to do."

"I *am* doing what I've always wanted to do. And, in case you hadn't noticed, I'm too young to retire."

Oh, he'd noticed all right. Noticed every damn thing about her, from the set of her mouth to the way her eyebrows rose and disappeared beneath her hair, bringing the dark bangs down until they were almost hanging into her eyes.

Why was she being this pigheaded about even talking about the sale? Most women he knew would like nothing better than to sit back and enjoy a wheelbarrow full of money that was being dumped into their laps.

But if it was work she was after, he could guarantee her that, as well.

"If you wanted to continue working here, we could easily make arrangements to that effect. You could stay on and manage the restaurant for us under Winfield's supervision for a very handsome salary."

Satisfied that he had neatly touched all the bases, he waited to hear her agree.

Was this man an idiot, or was he deliberately doing this to annoy her? Didn't he understand anything about family pride, about building something you could look back on with complete satisfaction? You couldn't do that with a bank account unless you had coins for blood.

The short laugh was filled with disdain. "Run my own place under Winfield's say-so?" She'd sooner run the business stark naked. "I don't think so. I don't need his say-so. I'm running it just fine without him."

Jared played one of the aces he held in his hand. "You're losing money."

He realized he'd made a tactical error as soon as he saw the expression on her face. She looked as if she'd been slapped.

How dare he throw that up to her? "Temporarily," she snapped. "And I'll thank you not to poke your nose into my business." Indignant pride filled her voice. "Besides, we'll come around again."

He indicated that he had no doubts about business picking up once more. But how long before that happened? And could she afford to wait?

"Winfield is large enough to absorb the costs until you do."

She didn't care if Winfield had pockets that could hide Jabba the Hutt. He wasn't going to get her restaurant into them.

"Very big of him," Demi said coldly. "The answer is still no."

Although her stand was definitely a roadblock to him, Jared had to admit that he liked her style. Still, he had to point out the obvious. "Are you big enough to absorb the costs?"

She thought of the note her father had taken out on the restaurant years ago. The one that was coming due all too soon. Somehow she'd find a way around it. And none of it concerned this man in her kitchen who was rooting for her to fail.

"This interview is over, Mr. Panetta. Now, maybe you didn't notice," she said, her voice becoming overly sweet, "but Guy, like all policemen, is wearing a gun. The safety's on right now, but, unlike the ownership of this restaurant, that's not a permanent thing." Rocking forward on her toes ever so slightly, she looked him right in the eye. "Did I also mention that I know how to fire a handgun?"

He had no idea whether or not she was serious, but something told him not to push it. Especially when she continued.

"Ever see a bullet wound, Mr. Panetta? It's a lot more gruesome than what you see on TV."

The door on the opposite end of the kitchen swung opened. Guy poked his head in, looking around for them. George pointed toward the rear.

"Everything okay in here?"

Demi took the opportunity to open the rear door. "Everything's fine, Guy. Mr. Panetta was just leaving." She placed her hand squarely on his shoulder. This time she didn't bother waiting until he took her hint.

"I—" Jared opened his mouth, then sucked in air as Demi suddenly shoved him backward out the opened door.

The door didn't remain open for long. Or unlocked. It wouldn't give when he tried it.

She'd won the first round, he thought with grudging admiration. But there were nine more to go before the championship bout was over. And the decision, he had no doubt, would go to him.

3

"Looks like you've got trouble, Demi." Lena's smile was slow and appreciative as she leaned in closer to Demi in the booth. The napkin in her hands remained unfolded as her eyes indicated the entrance. "Tall, Dark and Handsome is back."

Something had told Demi yesterday that she hadn't seen the last of him. Steeling herself, she turned in her seat toward the front of the restaurant. Jared was just walking in. Cradled in the crook of his arm was the lushest bouquet of roses she'd ever seen. Pink, like a baby's cheek.

For just the tiniest second, Demi could feel herself slipping as she looked at the flowers. The next moment, she'd completely banished the feeling. She knew what Panetta was up to. A three-year-old would have known what he was up to.

Of all the hokey, absurd, elementary stunts—

Demi sighed, irritated. She pushed the stack of freshly laundered and newly folded dark green napkins to one side of the table.

"More like Tall, Dark and Annoying."

The expression on Lena's face told Demi she didn't quite see it that way. Lena clearly seemed to have forgotten that she was engaged. "Gotta like a man who doesn't give up."

"No, I don't."

Lena had been right about one thing—this felt like trouble. And Demi didn't particularly want a witness who had all but announced her affiliation to the other side. Demi nodded to the left.

"Table seven looks like they're ready to order, Lena," she said pointedly. Reluctantly, Lena rose and made her way to the table.

Having dispensed Lena, Demi strode toward the interloper, loaded for bear. She meant to send him and his damn roses on their way as quickly as possible. She didn't need problems today. She had a banquet to think of.

Jared wasn't really up on his Greek mythology, but an artist's rendition he'd once seen stuck in his mind. The owner of Aphrodite looked like a petite version of Artemis, goddess of the hunt, as she purposefully walked toward him. Artemis, ready to slay the poacher for daring to tread on sacred land.

Jared smiled to himself. He supposed he was getting a bit carried away, but surrounded by all this atmosphere, it was difficult not to. He'd been with Winfield for seven years now, working his way up and helping Jack Winfield expand his holdings. Winfield, Inc., owned a number of restaurants in the county—fifteen at last count. All different, all with their own unique style and cuisine, yet Jared couldn't remember any of them ever having this kind of effect on him.

Once inside the small restaurant, it was as if he were transported beyond the confines of a growing city in Southern California. Beyond and back through time. Across the ages to a time when things were a hell of a lot simpler. And settled far more easily.

He reminded himself that it was the difficulty that kept things from getting dull for him. It was the challenge that kept his interest from wandering.

Right now he found his interest very narrowly focused. He liked his work. And it certainly didn't hurt that the woman who was his assignment this time around was exotically attractive and sparked his imagination.

As Demi reached him, Jared held out the bouquet to her.

Her eyes squarely on his, Demi deliberately pushed the flowers to one side. She wasn't going to be won over by a profusion of colorful vegetation. Damn it, she wasn't going to be won over at all, especially not by some pretty boy who thought he could toss a few well-worded compliments her way and have her eagerly signing on the dotted line.

Her heart-shaped face clouded. "Just what part of no are you having difficulty understanding, Mr. Panetta?"

He was about to remind her that they were supposed to be on a first-name basis, but never got the chance. She started poking him in the chest with a very sharp index finger, emphasizing each word she uttered.

"I said I wasn't interested in selling the restaurant under any circumstances and a few fat-cheeked little roses aren't going to make me change my mind."

He caught her hand easily in his. Her eyes widened in surprise. They were enormous, he thought. And beautiful. "I wouldn't insult your intelligence by trying to bribe you with roses." His voice was as calm as hers was filled with emotion.

Incensed, Demi yanked her hand free. "No?" She struggled to keep her voice low. She didn't care what he thought of her, but there were customers to consider. Past lunch, there were only a few patrons in the restaurant, and only one table of people whom she didn't know by sight. Still, there was no sense in sounding as if she were some ill-tempered shrew. Even if she felt like one right now. "Then just how would you insult my intelligence?"

"Not at all," he assured her with understated feeling. As if she hadn't already just dismissed them, Jared presented the roses to her. "These are to apologize."

Refusing to accept them, Demi crossed her arms before her.

"For what? Not that you don't have a lot to apologize for," she allowed, "but I prefer my apologies to be specific."

She had a way with words, he thought. Winfield

could use someone like her. If he survived first contact.

"For upsetting you."

He was the soul of sincerity. Had she been someone else, she might have been tempted to believe him. But Demi had been born suspicious.

"Believe me when I say that wasn't my intention," he continued.

"I wouldn't believe you if you told me the sky was blue." Still ignoring the roses, she looked at him contemptuously. "I know exactly what your intention was, just as I know exactly what your intention is now, Mr. Panetta."

"Jared," he corrected without missing a beat. "And just what do you think my intention is?"

Demi rolled her eyes. She had no idea why she was even bothering to talk to him. She certainly had better things to do.

"To pretend that you're an amicable guy so that I'll get to like you and let you somehow talk me into selling something that's been in the family for almost sixty years."

He'd known five minutes into their first meeting that it wasn't going to be anywhere near that easy. He smiled now at the simplistic scenario.

"Give me a little credit for having more brains than that, Demi. I know a woman of principle when I see her."

And she was that, which made the game that much more interesting, he mused. He wasn't trying to do anything underhanded. He was trying to win her over, not hoodwink her. If he used what was readily available to him, such as his charm, well, he couldn't be faulted for that any more than an accountant could be faulted for using his brains in completing his work. He was just using the talents he had at hand.

He was trying to snow her, she thought. Twisting around her own words to get what he wanted. Fat chance.

"Well, take a good look at this 'woman of principle' because you won't be seeing her for long." Hooking her arm through his, she abruptly escorted him back to the front entrance. "Thank you for visiting, Mr. Panetta. You'll understand when I say, 'Please don't stay in touch.'"

He stopped moving so suddenly, he threw her off balance. The quick, soft encounter as her body brushed against his was not lost on him. Neither was the sharp, almost electrical charge that accompanied it.

"I also wanted to pay for the dessert I had," he added.

Wasn't she ever going to be rid of him? "You had only half."

He nodded his agreement. "Which is another reason I'm back. I'd like to have the other half."

The lights were on, but there was obviously no one home. She almost felt sorry for him. But not quite. "We threw it away."

Unhindered by her hold, Jared stepped into the dining room again. "Then I'll just have to order another piece." He looked at her over his shoulder. "The taste of that one bite haunted me all night." Perhaps "haunted" was a little strong, but sampling the delicacy had stirred a craving within him for more.

Just as, he supposed suddenly, kissing Demetria Tripopulous might very well stir a craving for more. She had the kind of mouth that made a man stop in his tracks and begin to fantasize. Jared wondered if her lips ever stopped moving long enough for anyone to kiss her. He doubted it. Still, he would have liked to be the one to try. Just to see if he was right.

He heard hands being clapped together, accompanied by a low squeal of delight. "Oh, look who is back. Mr. Panetta."

The next moment, Demi's mother was joining them. Her eyes immediately alighted on the bouquet he was still holding. "And you brought Demetria flowers."

Like a miner trying to tunnel his way out of a cave-in, Jared gravitated to the light in the woman's eyes.

"I'm afraid she doesn't want them," he said with just the right touch of sadness. Then, turning, he presented the bouquet to Antoinette with a courtly inclination of his dark head. "Roses always look better in the arms of a lovely lady."

Oh, he was good, Demi thought. Almost too good. And that was very, very bad. One look told her that her mother had sunk into the pool of his oily words like a piece of paper weighed down by a rock.

"Oh, Mr. Panetta." Her mother blushed like a schoolgirl.

Jared shook his head in response. "Call me Jared, please."

Before she was through, she intended to call him son, and have him refer to her as Mother Tripopulous. Antoinette gave him a dazzling smile.

"Well, 'Jared-Please,' make yourself at home." With her free hand, she gestured toward a nearby booth.

Demi stared, dumbfounded. Her mother was flirting with the snake.

The snake smiled at her, satisfaction evident in his eyes, as he slid into the booth.

"Thank you." Turning, his eyes and his attention were all for her mother, but Demi would have sworn that she was the target of that studied, guileless look. "I came back for the baklava."

To Demi's further horror, her mother seemed to think nothing of sitting down in the booth and joining this troublemaker. She was taking to him as if he were a long-lost nephew, brought by the angels to her doorstep.

Didn't her mother know the difference between angels and devils?

"They always do," Antoinette confided with pride. "They did even before Demetria played around with the recipe. But now, it is our most popular item. Somehow she has found a way to make the perfect even more so."

Demi struggled to bank down the flood of color she felt rising to her cheeks as Jared's unabashed look slowly worked over her. She felt as if her clothes had suddenly vanished.

"Yes, she certainly has," he agreed with a smile that was nothing short of seductive.

"I don't have time for this," Demi retorted, turning on her heel. Maybe if she ignored him, he'd go away. At least she would be spared having to be in the same room with him. "The Forakis christening party is coming at four and there's still a lot of work to do in the kitchen."

"Send Lena out with two pieces of baklava," Antoinette called after her daughter.

Then she turned to study the young man sitting opposite her. She looked at him pointedly. "So, Jared, it is not that I do not appreciate roses, even secondhand ones, but you are going to need more than that if you intend to secure my daughter's attention."

He began to say something, but she waved it away. It was probably some half-truth at the very least. Young people never fared well when they were confronted.

"She needs a firm hand, my Demetria. Not to tame her, mind you, but to join with hers. Partners." She brought her hands together and laced them to illustrate her point. Her eyes searched his face and she liked what she saw. "She does not respect a man she can rule or intimidate. Like her father, may he rest in peace," she said, crossing herself to underscore her words, "she likes a partner who can outshout her on occasion."

A bittersweet, nostalgic smile crossed her face. It made her beautiful. The resemblance between mother and daughter was immediate.

"I am telling you this in case you are here for more than just a taste of the baklava." She winked at him broadly, her hand covering his in the way of a co-conspirator.

He was getting in a bit deeper than he'd intended. Jared debated how to play the cards he was holding. If he pretended to be interested in Demi, he knew that her mother would instantly be on his side. That kind of asset wasn't something to shrug off lightly. He felt confident he could convince the older woman that it was a smart move to sell the restaurant to Winfield. This was an old-fashioned family and the opinion of a parent, no matter what was said to the contrary, was still something to be reckoned with.

But using opportunities that came his way was one thing; being completely underhanded was another. He couldn't—wouldn't—do that. The trick here was being able to walk the fine line without losing his balance.

His silent debate was cut short by a resounding crash coming from the kitchen. It was immediately followed by a high-pitched scream.

"Excuse me. I will be right back," Antoinette promised him.

Moving with the ease of a young girl, she slid out

of the booth and hurried to the kitchen to see what was wrong. She was still clutching the roses.

It never occurred to Jared to hang back and wait for secondhand information. He was behind her by the time she pushed open the swinging door.

Pieces of shattered plates, like a jagged circle of sharks, surrounded the young woman he saw in the middle of the kitchen. She looked almost hysterical as she choked back a sob.

"I'm sorry, I'm sorry," she repeated over and over. As if the words could make the pieces come together again, making the plates whole. She was holding tightly on to her hand. Blood was oozing through the spaces between her fingers.

Demi stepped over the baklava that lay like fallen soldiers on the freshly scrubbed floor, casualties of circumstances beyond their control. Quickly she examined Eleanor's hand.

"Hold your arm up," she ordered, cupping Eleanor's elbow and pushing it toward the ceiling. "It'll help stop the bleeding." She looked around for her cousin as her mother began to soothe the waitress. Eleanor was shaking like a leaf. "George, get the first-aid kit for me from the back."

Jared saw George's expression at the same time that Demi did. Closer, Jared moved quickly enough to catch the cook before he passed out. His face was drained of all color.

Half dragging the younger man, Jared got him to a chair. "Sit down and put your head between your knees," he ordered. He looked up toward Demi. "Where's the kit?"

"In the office. In the back." Belatedly she realized he was going there. "I don't want you in my office," she called after him.

"I promise I won't take anything," he tossed over his shoulder. Was she always so suspicious, or was it just him? Obviously his charm was falling short of its mark, he thought. He had no idea why that amused him. It shouldn't. It did.

The office took him aback for a second. Organized to what some thought a fault, Jared shuddered at the chaos that greeted him.

She ran the restaurant from here? It was a wonder that anything was ever accomplished if this paper-littered alcove was any indication of how she operated. It was the kind of mess that made him want to close the door and just walk away.

But that wasn't going to locate the first-aid kit for him. Moving things gingerly around, Jared began to search the desk. Since the office was small, there weren't that many places to look.

He found the first-aid kit on his third try, in the bottom drawer of a desk that had seen better times. Perhaps better decades.

"Got it," he called as he hurried out of the room. He flipped open the box and began rummaging through the contents.

"Took you long enough," Demi muttered.

Her arm wrapped around Eleanor in mute support,

Demi held out her hand toward Jared expectantly. Her hand remained empty. Surprised, she looked behind her. Jared had the blue box opened on the counter and was taking things out.

Armed with what he needed, he approached the young woman. "Here, let me see that," he coaxed gently, as gently as if he were speaking to Theresa, his five-year-old. Obediently, the woman extended her hand. "What's your name?" he asked as he swabbed the jagged cut with peroxide.

Her eyes followed his every move. "Eleanor," she whispered.

"That's a very nice name, Eleanor," he said softly. He tossed the bloodied cotton ball into the garbage. "I'm Jared."

"Thank you." Eleanor hiccuped as she tried to get her sobs under control. "I'm so sorry, Demi. I didn't mean to drop it. I was trying not to sneeze," she explained timidly.

"Of course you didn't mean to drop it," Demi said. Why was Eleanor reacting this way? Was the woman afraid of her? Had she really turned into some kind of ogre without realizing it?

"I'll pay for it," she promised.

Demi didn't care for the look Jared slanted her. It said the very things she was thinking. "Don't even think about it."

The first Band-Aid he'd applied to Eleanor's wound was already beginning to turn red. "There's so much blood," Eleanor whispered.

56 THE OFFER SHE COULDN'T REFUSE

"It usually looks a lot worse than it is," he assured her. Tearing off the wrapper from a couple more butterfly Band-Aids, he applied them one by one to the zigzag wound. "You shouldn't have tried to pick up the pieces with your hand."

Eleanor bit her lower lip. "I didn't think."

"Natural mistake." One more Band-Aid and he was done. He gently slipped his hand from the woman's. "I think you might need stitches. It's too close to call. Best to have it looked at by a doctor."

"Stitches," she squeaked fearfully.

He grinned. "They don't hurt that much. And maybe you won't need them. Don't worry, you'll be all right. But there'll be no waitressing for you today."

Just who the hell did he think he was, Superdoctor? "Did your X-ray vision tell you that?" Demi wanted to know.

"Demetria," her mother chided.

It irritated Demi no end that her mother was still holding Jared's damn roses. And worse yet, the next moment Jared came to her defense.

"That's all right." He looked at Demi, wiping off his hands. "No, my common sense tells me that," he answered Demi's question. "That, and a crash course in first aid at the local Y."

She held that highly suspect. Corporate vultures like Jared Panetta didn't go slumming at the Y and take courses in anything. That was for working-class people like her.

"And why would you take a crash course in first aid? To deal with the heart attacks you instigate?"

If she was trying to get him to lose his temper, she was going to be disappointed. He hadn't lost his temper in a long, long time. Not since Gloria had walked out on him and Theresa.

"No, to be prepared in case something happened to my little girl. I like knowing I can deal with anything that might come up." Although, in this case, he had a feeling that there was no crash course at the Y that would prepare him for one Demetria Tripopulous.

Antoinette looked surprised. Her face softened as she related to him, one parent to another. "You have a daughter?"

He nodded. "Theresa. She's five."

"Do you have any pictures?" Antoinette asked eagerly, temporarily forgetting about Eleanor.

"Plenty."

The wallet he produced from his pants pocket fairly bulged with photographs of his daughter. As he flipped it open to one, even Eleanor oohed over the little girl captured with ice cream over her sunny face.

Demi looked, too, despite herself. His daughter looked like him, except her hair was a soft, silky blond. An angel.

Demi was beginning to feel as if the deck was stacked. Panetta seemed to just be reeling them in with everything he did.

"Any pictures of your wife?" Demi asked pointedly, congratulating herself on effectively bringing an end to this session of show-and-tell.

Jared's face darkened as he returned the wallet to his pocket. "No. I took those out."

Why? she caught herself wondering. But that was probably just what he wanted her to do—to wonder about him. To wonder and be subtly drawn in to the web he was weaving.

It wasn't going to happen, she promised him silently, her innate curiosity notwithstanding.

"Well, this impromptu sharing period is all very lovely, but I'm down one waitress, my cousin the cook is sitting with his head between his knees and I have a party of a hundred and seventy-five people coming to celebrate a christening in less than two hours."

"I'm okay." George's voice came up to her weakly from floor level. "Just give me a minute. Has she stopped bleeding?" He raised his head slowly from between his knees.

Demi rolled her eyes. No one would ever accuse George of taking after his namesake, Saint George the dragon slayer.

"Yes, she's stopped bleeding. You can come up for air now." Demi turned to her mother. "Ma, get rid of those damn roses and drive Eleanor to the emergency room, then come right back. I'm going to need you here in the kitchen with Theo and George. We've got a lot more Kreatopittes to make. George, take a few deep breaths and then get a broom and clean up this floor. I don't want any more accidents." She shifted toward the other waitress. "Lena, I want you to get back out there and cover for Eleanor. I'll be out to help you as soon as I can." After two weeks of slow afternoons, Murphy's Law dictated that this would be the day that they would be swamped.

Jared closed the lid on the first-aid kit. "What do you want me to do?"

"That's easy." She pushed past him as everyone scattered to comply with her instructions. "Get out of my way."

This was definitely not going to be a piece of cake, Jared thought as he followed her to the small office. He felt himself loving it.

When she looked up at him accusingly, he elaborately replaced the first-aid kit, then firmly closed the bottom drawer.

"What are you going to do?" he wanted to know.

Maybe the best way to deal with him was to ignore him as much as possible. She began to rummage through the different piles of papers, looking for her address book. "About what?"

"Your party of one hundred and seventy-five." He doubted she could wait on them with just Lena. He'd seen the way the other waitress moved, like glue in a container. And quick though she was, Demi couldn't hope to do it all herself.

Her temper threatened to get the best of her. "Not that it's any business of yours, but I intend to handle it. All I have to do is find my book with the number of the temp agency in it."

She shoved another stack over and found nothing. She began patting through the papers, looking for a telltale five-by-seven lump. It continued to elude her.

Demi smacked the top of the table with the flat of her hand. "Damn, it was right here." She looked at him accusingly. "Did you put it someplace?"

"The tornado had already struck by the time I got to your office. You could lose Texas in here and not know it." The corners of his mouth lifted engagingly. "I'd ask you how you ever manage to find anything in this mess, but I think I already have my answer."

What had she ever done to deserve this? "Yes, you do, and that answer revolves around the word *no*." At the end of her patience, she turned to the file cabinet, only to find her way blocked. She stared him down. "Now, unless you want to be bodily removed, I'd suggest you leave."

He wasn't ready to move just yet, not until she satisfied his curiosity. "And just who would be doing the bodily removing?"

Demi squared her shoulders, rising to her full height of barely five-two. "Don't let my size fool you. The women in my family are very strong."

After a momentary debate of weighing the pros and cons of the physical contact, he stepped aside. But his smile remained intact.

"Not that I don't think that might be an interesting and very possibly pleasant experience, but I think you're being a little too hasty about throwing me out."

"You're entitled to your opinion, but mine's the one that counts." She shoved the last drawer shut with a resounding bang. "Damn it, where is that book?"

Knowing it was a little like sticking his head into the lion's cage, he still turned her around to face him. "You don't need the book."

What was he talking about? "Of course I need the book." She shrugged his hands off her shoulders. "I don't remember the agency's telephone number."

"You don't have to call the agency to send someone. I'll help." He'd done some waitering and bartendering while he'd been in college. It was at one of these functions that he had first met Winfield.

It was one of the few times in her life that Demi remembered ever being speechless. But she was. Completely.

4

"Did I just hear you correctly?" Demi stared at Jared in disbelief. Just what the hell did this man think he was up to? "Are you volunteering to be a waiter at this evening's banquet?"

Shoulders that were a little too broad for a comfortable off-the-rack fit rose and fell casually in response to her incredulous tone.

"Why not? It's honest work and a break for you. You can't get any better rates than free."

He really had to think she was a simpleton to fall for this Good Samaritan act of his. "Why are you doing this—as if I didn't know."

If she was trying to get under his skin, she was going to have to do better than that, Jared thought. He was the soul of innocence as he answered. "Because you and I got off on the wrong foot and I want to make amends. Besides, there is the small matter of the half-eaten dessert I didn't pay for."

Now he was trying flattery again. The man bounced around like an energized handball in a concrete room, hoping, undoubtedly, to tire her out.

It was evident he didn't know who and what he was up against, Demi thought.

"My baklava is good, Mr. Panetta, but it doesn't warrant three hours' work in lieu of payment." Her gaze met his as she issued her warning. "You're not going to break me down by trying to be nice."

The same slow, lazy smile he'd worn earlier slipped over Jared's lips and into her with annoying ease. "I'm not 'trying,' Demi. I *am* nice."

Yeah, right. Nice. He was here to get her to sell the restaurant to his firm any way he could. That included, or maybe even encouraged, subterfuge. Well, she wasn't born yesterday or the day before that, and she definitely wasn't a fifty-seven-year-old woman desperate to marry off a daughter she feared was passing the prime childbearing years of her life.

"That might work on my mother, but she's been sheltered." Demi looked at him pointedly. "I, however, haven't been."

God help him, he was beginning to get a kick out of this. It was like a game of mental chess. He couldn't remember when he'd enjoyed his work more.

"I'm not the big, bad wolf, Demi."

He wasn't sure just what possessed him. Maybe it was even a tactical mistake on his part, but it was one he couldn't seem to help. Jared brushed his fingers against her hair. Just the barest ends as they swirled a couple of inches shy of her shoulders. He needed to satisfy at least that much of his growing curiosity about her.

64   THE OFFER SHE COULDN'T REFUSE

Her hair felt thick and lush. Just as he thought it would.

To his surprise, Demi didn't jerk her head back. It was the look in her eyes that made him drop his hand. It was as if she knew he was going to do that and he'd just proven her right.

With effort, Demi succeeded in keeping out of her voice the quiver that was traveling through her body. "Wolves come in many shapes and sizes. They don't all have a long snout, fur and long legs."

Touché. As he stepped back, Jared's eyes drifted over the length of her compact, firm body. "Speaking of legs, yours are very nice."

The look was so sensual, she could swear she felt it pass along her body. For a second, just the tiniest measure of time, she savored the effect. It was a mistake. It allowed Jared to know he'd scored a point, however small.

Damn him, anyway.

She wasn't going to let him get to her. It was just what he was trying to do. To get to her and to undermine her.

"My legs are none of your business, Mr. Panetta. And my *business* is none of your business, either."

Striding on the long legs he'd noticed the first moment he'd watched her walk away from him, Demi marched through the kitchen into the dining hall. She looked around as if she were trying to locate someone. And then he saw her smile.

"Bruno, want to make a quick ten bucks an hour?"

The man she was talking to was seated at the far table, just in front of the booth where her grandfather and his friend were still staring at the regal, and as yet unmoved, chess pieces.

Bruno looked up from his newspaper when she addressed him. In Jared's opinion, he looked big and clumsy, more apt to drop dishes than to carry them. It was obvious she was getting desperate.

"Sure. When?"

Saved, Demi thought, relieved. "Tonight at six. I need a waiter."

The cheerful expression faded from his large-boned face. Bruno looked at her sheepishly. "Gee, Demi, I wish I could, but I've got to meet Estelle this evening. She's taking me to her folks' house for dinner." He looked as if he equated the ordeal with a slow, painful death.

Demi nodded. "Thanks anyway." Avoiding looking in Jared's direction, she scanned the dining room for any volunteers among the regulars.

Everyone she asked had something else to do or somewhere else to be. There were no takers and she didn't have time to call around. Even if she found her telephone book, the temp agency probably wouldn't be able to send anyone in time. She was stuck.

"Offer still stands," Jared told her cheerfully when she turned around.

She'd almost bumped into him. Annoyed, she stepped back. What was he up to now, understudying her shadow? "Do you have to stand so close?"

She looked ruffled, and unless he missed his guess, it only partially had to do with finding a replacement for Eleanor. Ever so slowly, he was gaining an advantage. Jared silently congratulated himself.

"No, that's a bonus. For me."

He wasn't exaggerating completely. She did smell good. Amid the combined heavenly aromas seductively drifting out from the kitchen was something arousingly different when he stood close to her. Something musky that was immediately absorbed by every pore in his body.

She didn't like the way he was looking at her. As if she was the very last piece of baklava left on the dessert cart. She liked the way she was reacting to that look even less.

Struggling with the unsettled feeling that insisted on washing over her, Demi took refuge in business. "Do you have any experience?"

"Some."

When the smile on his lips widened, she had to curb the temptation to give him a swift kick. She wasn't about to listen to a recitation of the women he'd had. "I meant at being a waiter."

The smile, along with the tone, turned innocent. Only his eyes continued to be amused. "That's what I meant, too."

The hell he did. She knew what he was up to. He was mocking her. Well, let him if that was what kept him happy. She'd have the last laugh in this little drama. He wasn't deluding her. It wasn't her he was interested in, it was the restaurant. He obviously thought the way to secure her signature on the dotted line was to play up to her. Okay, fine, she might as well make the most of the opportunity that presented itself. Having thought it over, she'd decided that he wouldn't try to sabotage the party. There was nothing to gain by that if he was trying to play up to her.

"All right," she relented. "I'm in a bind and I could use you. Pays the same. Eight dollars an hour."

Not that he intended to take it, but the pay was *not* the same. "You were going to give him ten." He nodded toward Bruno.

He wasn't on the job yet and he was already challenging her authority. "I offered him ten because he's experienced and I knew what I was getting with him. As far as I'm concerned, you are a pig in a poke." She sincerely hoped she wasn't going to regret this. But her back was to the wall. What else could she do? "All right, I want it clear that you do exactly as I tell you to. Oh, and one more thing—you break anything, you pay for it."

That sounded fair. It was her tone that didn't. "I can see why you have so many people clamoring to work for you." Amusement crept from his eyes to highlight his entire face. "You must have to beat them off with a stick."

Right now she was contemplating beating him with a stick. A very large stick.

It annoyed her that she was in a position where she needed him. But even she knew her limitations, and she couldn't be everywhere at once. She needed at least four extra hands besides hers serving food and drinks.

Demi never missed a beat. "And since you're working for me, I'll thank you to keep any comments you might have to yourself."

Obliging her, Jared saluted smartly. "Your wish is my command."

Demi shut her eyes, biting her tongue. With all her heart, she wished that Eleanor hadn't picked today to be so clumsy. But she had, and Demi was just going to have to work with it.

Opening her eyes again, she looked at Jared. She might as well put him to work setting up the banquet room before people began arriving. But first, she had to see to things in the kitchen.

"Wait here until I call you," she instructed tersely.

"With baited breath." Pleased, he sat down in the booth he'd shared with her mother. "By the way, can I have one of those little desserts while I wait?"

Couldn't he even remember what it was called? "Baklava."

"Baklava," Jared repeated, wrapping his tongue around the word as if he were caressing a lover.

Demi had to concentrate to shake free of the feeling he was too damn successful in creating.

"You're a waiter now. Get it yourself," she tossed over her shoulder, afraid that if she looked at him, he'd see the effect he was having on her.

His voice drifted after her. "But I'm not on duty until you call me, right?"

Demi shoved the door open with the flat of her hand, annoyed. This was *not* shaping up to be one of her better days.

Demi fully expected Murphy's Law to go into fourth gear once the Forakis christening party got under way. After all, she was working with an unknown. What was worse, try as she might, she was depending on him to some extent, and he knew it.

But Murphy's Law had been repealed, at least for the evening. There were no further mishaps in the kitchen, or out of it. Things went amazingly smoothly as she, Lena and Jared went in and out of the banquet room, weaving through a crowd that seemed to be perpetually in motion. Because they were constantly milling about, there appeared to be twice as many people as had been quoted. But that was only an illusion. The music, the dancing and the noise all contributed to the feeling that the banquet hall was filled beyond capacity.

She worked hard, moved fast. And felt wonderful. Demi never felt as alive as she was in the center of a crowded room filled with people eating her food.

When her feet began to ache into the second hour, she barely noticed. It was something she would deal with later, after everyone had gone home and she and the others had cleaned up. Right now, there were people to accommodate.

She seemed bent on everyone having a good time, Jared thought, watching her. Whenever possible, he'd been observing Demi in action. He was beginning to understand why the restaurant had the reputation that it did. Demi seemed to be everywhere, exchanging bits of conversation with about two thirds of the people at the banquet. All while making sure that everything was running like the proverbial Swiss watch.

Jared paused to look at her as he finished mixing the last batch of drinks that had been requested. He placed them on the bar beside a half-empty bottle of wine. She was positively glowing, he thought.

The glow of what his father had once referred to as "honest toil."

God, he hadn't thought of that term for a long time. Or of his father, he realized.

He supposed it was only natural. The family-oriented restaurant conjured up images of his own family, long since gone their separate ways. His mother, a widow now, had moved up north to be closer to her sister. His brother and sister lived in different cities these days. It had been a while since they'd all gotten together. What, four, five years now? He wasn't sure. Maybe he'd give his mother a call later this week. Put Theresa on. He knew his mother would get a kick out of talking to her granddaughter.

Jared roused himself. This wasn't the time to get nostalgic. He was here to accomplish something. To find a chink in that coat of armor Demi wore like a second skin, and work at it until he got it to come off. If she was just willing to listen to reason, he knew he could make her see the merits of selling to Winfield rather than working herself into a frazzle trying to run a business.

Not that she looked frazzled, he noted, wiping the water spots off the counter. That in itself seemed incredible, given the fact that she seemed to be everywhere at once. Every time he turned around, she was either checking on the food, helping to serve it or mingling with the guests.

Eavesdropping, he'd discovered that she ran the kitchen like a drill sergeant, even ordering Theo around. But everyone accepted it and seemed to take it in stride. And no one took offense.

Placing a tray with empty glasses on the counter, Demi came around to Jared's side of the small, portable bar she'd put up in the room earlier.

"You're behind with the drinks." Finding fault with him heartened her. Up until now, he seemed to be handling everything almost too well. "Need a hand?"

Maybe it was his imagination, but for once she didn't sound as if she absolutely loathed him. Progress.

He offered her a contrite smile. "Sorry, I was just watching you in action and I guess I got caught up in the tailwind." He took out more glasses from beneath the counter and started pouring wine into them. "You always move around this fast?"

"Just when I'm awake."

Loading the glasses onto the tray faster than he was pouring, Demi elbowed Jared out of the way. She reached beneath the counter for a bottle of anisette. They were running low, she thought, wondering if she should send Lena to get another bottle.

She poured two fingers' worth of the clear liquid into a glass. "Things don't get done by themselves."

"Apparently," he said. Demi began to pick up the tray. "I'll do that," he told her. Very carefully he removed her hands before she had the opportunity to lift the tray. "It's what I signed on for, remember?" he added when she looked at him in surprise.

Inclining his head toward her, he picked up the tray and went to make the rounds.

Demi reached for the glass of anisette and took the tiniest of sips as she watched Jared weaving through the crowd. Watched, too, as he garnered more than his share of appreciative looks from the women.

Nothing had changed. She didn't trust him. Not any further than she could throw that handsome, six-foot-something body of his. But she had to admit, she did like watching it move away from her. The man had a hell of a butt.

Stunned at the direction her thoughts were taking, Demi pushed the glass of anisette aside. She hurried back to the kitchen to check on the main course.

The warm flush that insisted on winding its way through her body only became more intense as she entered the kitchen.

Theo looked up as he closed the oven door. "So, how is he doing?"

Demi shrugged. It took her a second to remember why she'd come here. Panetta was definitely having a bad effect on her, she thought moodily. Was that why he'd volunteered? To make her crazy? "He hasn't broken anything yet."

George floured the top of the worktable before he began making the next batch of pastries. He slanted a look toward his cousin. "I saw the way Melina Planteous was looking at him when the party started. I'd say he's got her sewed up if he wants her."

"Melina?" She hooted. Jared and Melina—now that made a picture. "Well, she's welcome to him." For her money, they deserved each other. Melina was a twenty-four-carat gold digger. There'd be poetic justice in the two of them getting together.

So why didn't the thought give her any comfort?

Demi blew out a long breath, her hands making fists on her hips.

"What he wants, ladies and gentlemen," she announced in case anyone was being taken in by Jared's little volunteer act, "is the restaurant, and don't you forget it. That's why he's putting on this whole act. Why should he help us?" she wanted to know. "The man doesn't even know us."

"Maybe this will give him the opportunity to get to know us," Theo pointed out.

Demi smiled patiently at her grandfather. The man had a simple, kind heart. He didn't understand devious people. That was for her to deal with. And deal with it she intended.

But for now she allowed her grandfather his illusion that there was good in everyone. "If he wants to help out, fine. As long as he doesn't mess up our system, he can help. But that doesn't get him any closer to his goal."

"What if his goal isn't the restaurant?"

Demi turned around to look at her mother. She would say that. But her mother saw only what she wanted to see: a potential son-in-law in every man.

Demi opened the oven door, determined to make her own assessment of the main course. "Of course it's the restaurant."

Antoinette wiped her hands on her apron, her eyes on Demi. "And what if he is interested in you?"

Demi sighed, closing the oven door. The lamb was progressing well. She, however, was not. They'd been through this already.

Trying to talk sense into her, Demi placed her hands on her mother's shoulders in a mute plea for support. "Ma, please, not now. He's not interested in me. He just wants to get his hands on the restaurant for his boss, the almighty Winfield Monopoly."

Lena walked in on the last part of the minidebate. She set her empty tray on the edge of the worktable, eyeing Demi. "Maybe, but I'd say that's not all he'd like to get his hands on."

Vindicated, Antoinette gestured at the younger woman with a triumphant sweep of her hand.

"See, Lena agrees with me. She has eyes. You," she lamented, "you are like your father." Antoinette shook her head sorrowfully. "You see nothing but work, work, work."

She'd had enough of this. Demi wiped her hands and swiftly loaded several orders of freshly baked bread onto her tray.

"That's because we have bills, bills, bills, Ma. Not to mention a very hefty note coming due from the bank." She looked at the woman pointedly. "Somebody has to take care of business around here." Her mother was a babe in the wood when it came to figures in a column. Her understanding of finances ended with the amount of money she found in her wallet.

"You tell 'em, kiddo," Theo encouraged, his thick Greek accent incongruent with the American slang.

He had a weak spot in his heart for his only granddaughter. Far too busy working to notice his children when they were growing up, he'd tried to make up for what he had missed by being part of Demi and Guy's formative years. And so far he was well pleased with the results he'd seen.

"Thank you." Demi kissed her grandfather's grizzled cheek. At least someone was on her side, she thought, walking out.

"You did well," Demi said grudgingly.

Jared looked over his shoulder, surprised. He hadn't heard her walk up behind his chair. He'd thought he was alone in the banquet room. The party had finally broken up half an hour ago, running two hours over. He'd seen a heavy-set, florid-faced older man he'd assumed was the head of the large, sprawling clan slip Demi a wad of money earlier. It was to buy them a little extra time, Lena had explained to him when he asked.

Jared had a strong hunch Demi would have allowed them to remain even without the added money.

The bits and pieces of conversation he'd picked while serving and clearing, bits and pieces he'd hoped would ultimately help him when he tried to convince her to sell again, confirmed the preliminary check he'd run himself on her business. Demi knew how to run a restaurant efficiently, but she allowed her heart to get in the way of accounts due. It gained her gratitude and a growing number of friends, but didn't put a dent in the debts that were mounting somewhere on her desk. Growing like mushrooms in the dark.

He wondered if she even knew they were there. Probably not, given the condition of that claustrophobia-inducing room.

He smiled up at her. It'd been a long time since he'd felt so physically tired. Even workouts at the gym hadn't produced this kind of exhaustion. This was the first time he'd sat down in over five hours. Demi, he noted, had been on her feet just as long. In heels. And she was still standing.

"You say that as if you expected me to break every dish in the place."

She shrugged. "Not every dish. Besides, I told you earlier you'd have to pay for them if you did. I wasn't worried."

He saw what looked like a smile playing on her lips. Nice, he thought. A smile looked nice on her. "You looked too busy to be worried about me."

And there was why he wouldn't win, she thought in tired satisfaction. He underestimated her. "You're wrong. I always watch my back."

He pretended to lean around her to look at it himself, then raised his eyes to hers.

"Neat trick. You'll have to teach it to me sometime. I'd say that would be anatomically tiring. How about I watch your back for you for a while?" His eyes teased her. "It's a very nice back to watch."

Her brow rose. She had to be careful. She must really be tired. Panetta was beginning to sound charming to her. But as long as she knew his motives, she'd be all right.

"You're the reason I'm watching it." Maybe it was because she felt so tired, but she couldn't seem to keep the smile from her lips. "You always flirt with everyone you try to take over?"

He rose to his feet. His body just missed brushing against hers. Jared silently lamented the extra space. It would have been nice to feel her against him, even fleetingly. Maybe even safer that way.

He looked down into her face now. "No, flirting isn't part of the job description."

It was getting warm again. She was going to have

to take a look at the thermostat and see what was wrong with it. "But deception is."

"I'm not deceiving you, Demi," he said softly. "I said I was a nice guy and I am."

She felt as if her breath had suddenly lost its way. "How nice?"

The look in his eyes made her even warmer. "What did you have in mind?"

She stepped back. She had to. All the air was gone from where she'd been standing. "The kitchen needs cleaning."

It took him a moment to regroup. Her answer wasn't what he'd expected.

"Okay," he allowed gamely. "Just let me call my daughter and say good-night and I'll get right on it."

Demi waved him back before he had a chance to go to her office and use her phone. A man who remembered to call his daughter before she went to bed at night couldn't be all bad. Even if Demi wanted him to be.

"I was just kidding. Go home to your daughter, Mr. Panetta," she told him, sighing. "You did your part."

He turned and this time, he did brush against her. The resulting spark smoldered until it ignited something else within him. He searched her face, wondering if what he felt was just his imagination. Or if she'd felt it, too.

"Do you think that you could find it in your heart to call me Jared?"

She slowly moved her head from side to side, held fast by the look in his eyes. "No."

"What can you find it in your heart to call me?"

His smile coaxed an image from the recesses of her mind. An image of him holding her. She tried to banish it.

But when he slipped his hands around her waist, she didn't back away. "You don't want to know."

"Yes," he said, his arms tightening just enough to make her move closer to him, "I do."

Demi swallowed. *Move, damn it,* she warned herself. She didn't listen.

"An oily snake."

"Ouch, that's a cruel one." Linking his fingers with hers, Jared took her hand and slowly ran it through his hair. "See, dry. No oil."

A feeling swirled through her. A feeling that quickened in places she didn't want quickening. Tired. She was definitely tired. Otherwise, she would have never been here, in this position. In his arms.

With his lips coming far too close to hers for comfort.

And, if she hadn't been so damn tired, she would have certainly had more sense than to be standing up on her toes to cut the last bit of distance between them.

But she was, and she did.

And as soon as she did, she knew there was going to be hell to pay.

5

If this was hell, it certainly wasn't the one she'd been taught about as a child. That one, an ancient priest had warned her and the other children in her class, was comprised of fire and brimstone, reserved for the wicked of heart.

This wasn't like that at all.

Not that there wasn't fire, or at least heat, because there was. Lots and lots of heat. So much so that Demi felt as if she were going to melt right here in his arms. Any minute now, he was going to find himself trying to hold on to a puddle instead of a woman.

Her heart pounding rapidly, Demi slanted her mouth avidly against his. Passion surged through her as she lost all feeling in her legs.

Didn't matter. She didn't need them. She was holding on to him.

No, not hell, heaven, she amended as she completely lost her way and herself in the bargain. Very definitely heaven. Heaven with a broken thermostat.

She felt like a tuning fork that had been struck on the side of a cast-iron cannon; every bone, every muscle, every single fiber in her body was vibrating madly as Demi clung to his arms. Vaguely she realized that she was trying to rally enough strength to push away, but she wasn't entirely sure why.

Why would anyone push away from heaven?

Framing her face between his hands, Jared deepened the kiss.

Pleasure spilled over him. It drew him further and further into the kiss, into a wonder he couldn't begin to understand or even describe to himself. His resistance to it was like a handkerchief being dropped on top of a grape juice stain. More and more of the stain crept into the fabric until all of it was completely consumed with it.

Consumed with her.

Resistance, if he even had enough brain power to contemplate it, was futile.

He gave up all attempts at thinking clearly. Jared wrapped his arms around her. Whether it was to bring Demi closer to him or to seal himself to her, he wasn't sure.

What he was sure of was that he wanted more of whatever it was he was sampling. Infinitely more. His thirst wasn't quenched, it was merely whetted.

She made him feel like a man walking out of a tomb, into the light. He'd been buried too soon. He was still alive, very much alive.

A door slammed somewhere in the distance. Maybe even in another world. The sound penetrated their world only slowly.

"Demetria, do you want me to lock up?" The question, guilelessly posed, was followed by an abrupt, deafening silence.

Theo's voice dropped on her like a bucket of cold water, making her gasp. Demi jerked away from Jared, pushing him back for good measure. She could feel her heart pounding in her chest, in her throat, even in her ears. This was *not* good.

Theo looked from one to the other, realizing only belatedly, that he had walked in on something.

"Oh, I see. You are already locked up." He raised his hamlike hands to ward off his own words. "Excuse an old man, I make a mistake. I see nothing." He began to back out of the banquet room, taking small, cautious steps. His hands remained raised. "The doctor, he says I should have glasses, but me, I say no. I see what I need to see, nothing more," he assured them. He turned, his hand on the doorknob. "So, I do not see this."

Oh, Lord, not only had she done something incredibly stupid, but she had done it in front of a witness.

"Theo—"

Her grandfather's name came out in a squeak. Demi cleared her throat, trying again, not having a clue what to say to him. All she was aware of was that the rat next to her had the gall to grin at her dilemma.

"Theo, I—we—that is—" The words came out no better without the squeak.

"Yes." Her grandfather's broad, amused smile

lifted his bushy mustache. "I know." His eyes were twinkling. "I will go now." He left before she could make a move to stop him.

Annoyed, frustrated and flustered, Demi dragged her hand through her hair. Why had Theo have to pick this moment to walk in? Why hadn't he just gone home the way she'd told him to? And why the hell had she allowed Panetta to kiss her when she knew what kind of a snake in the grass he was?

And worst of all, why had she enjoyed it?

Her hair fell back against her face like a swinging, black mop. "Well, that's going to be impossible to explain."

Maybe it was a good thing the old man had walked in when he did. Otherwise, Jared wasn't sure he could have readily stopped what they were on the edge of having happen. Now he'd never know, but it was probably better that way. He didn't want to get into any sticky, unethical areas.

Because his body still felt relatively unstable, Jared leaned a hip against the portable bar. He nodded toward the door Theo had gone through.

"Do you always explain to your grandfather what you do?"

Angry with herself, with succumbing so easily to what she viewed as a calculated act, Demi turned her anger on the only available target in the room. She pivoted on her heel to face Jared.

"I haven't had to explain myself to anyone for a long time. It's just that I choose to let them—my family—in on my life." Her tongue was getting all twisted in her mouth. Just like her thoughts were. "I mean—"

She gave up all attempts at a civilized conversation. "Damn it, Panetta, why did you have to go and do that for?" she demanded hotly. For a moment, when she'd walked in just now, she'd thought perhaps she'd been too hard on him. Now she knew she hadn't been hard enough. "I was actually beginning to think I might maybe, just maybe, like you the tiniest little bit."

Talk about trying to squeeze out a token drop, he thought with a grin. She was certainly back in form. "Was the kiss really that bad?"

"No." The response was automatic. Too automatic. "Yes." But that wasn't fair, either. And she'd always been fair, even to the enemy. "That wasn't what I was referring to. I mean—"

What *did* she mean? she thought angrily. Striving for calm, she took a deep breath. She felt as if all her systems had been scrambled. Demi looked up at him. She was just going to say this once and he had better get it straight.

"I'm not going to fall all over myself and sell the restaurant to you just because your kiss temporarily disoriented me, any more than I would because you helped me out tonight or because you brought me a damn bunch of roses." None of that was going to work on her. It wasn't. She wasn't the least little bit affected by any of it.

Except maybe in the worst possible way.

The smile was much too intimate, much too warm as it spread slowly on his lips. His eyes never left hers. "Did I?"

Demi blinked, trying to get her bearings. Were they in the same conversation? She was railing at him and he looked as if he were a cat falling headfirst into a vat of cream. "Did you what?"

He wanted to touch her. *Really* touch her. Jared clenched his hands and shoved them into his pockets. They remained clenched. "Temporarily disorient you?"

Demi's mouth dropped open. She drew a breath, knowing it was wiser to take stock before answering immediately. Cursing at him and his lineage was not going to accomplish anything—even though it might give her a temporary rush of satisfaction.

"Figure of speech," she bit off.

"Oh." He nodded as if he believed her. It wasn't any figure of speech that he was aware of. "Well." His eyes washed over her, silently telling her he knew she was lying. But at least one of them could tell the truth. "I guess I just might borrow that same figure of speech myself. Because you did. Temporarily disorient me," he added when she just stared at him as if she hadn't a clue what he was talking about.

Demi swallowed. She was not, *not,* going to kiss him again, although everything within her begged her to. "That daughter you wanted to say good-night to—"

"Theresa?"

"Theresa," she repeated, slowly nodding. Knowing if she nodded her head any faster, it just might spin off into oblivion, along with what was left of her brain.

"What about her?" he prodded when she didn't say anything further.

He probably thought she was some kind of an idiot. Or, at the very least, someone nobody had ever kissed before. That galvanized her.

Demi drew herself up. "Go home to her, Panetta. Say good-night in person." She paused, then added, "Little girls like that."

Something in the way she said it caught his attention. He tried to imagine her as a little girl and couldn't. Couldn't think of her in any other way than a firebrand who stirred him.

"Did you?"

She shook her head. "I don't know. I was always asleep by the time my dad came home."

He only nodded, as if he understood more than she was willing to let him. "You're right. I'd better go home." He walked toward the door, then turned to look at her again. "I'll see you."

"God, I hope not," she muttered.

Almost involuntarily, she ran the tips of her fingers over her lips as she watched his shadow disappear into the darkness.

Ever since she'd been a little girl, she'd turned to cooking whenever she was upset. She cooked to change the charged energy roaming around within her into something positive and productive.

She'd been in the restaurant's kitchen since 5:00 a.m. this morning.

Augmenting the day's menu, Demi created a special-of-the-day out of the lamb that had been left over from last night's party. Unable to sleep, she had to do something with herself besides think about Jared and rehash their last ten minutes together over and over again.

She didn't care for the knowing look she saw in her grandfather's eyes when he walked in through the back entrance at eight.

Shrugging out of the jacket she'd bought for him two Christmases ago, he hung it on the coatrack in the corner. His dark eyes swept over the array of food on the counter. "You are here early."

She lifted her chin defensively, ready to get into it if he wanted to make something of her motives. "So are you."

His reason was simple. "I thought I would get a cup of coffee and have it in peace before Alex comes in. That man talks and talks and takes away all the pleasure out of a good cup of coffee." He kibitzed for a moment, looking over her shoulder. "What are you doing?"

A flip answer rose to her lips, then quickly disappeared. She hadn't been raised to be flippant to Theo. "Cooking."

He nodded, as if her reply confirmed his guess. "So, how did we do last night?"

Here at least she was on safe ground. Demi stopped wrapping the grape leaves around the meat mixture and turned around to face him.

"Very well. Mr. Forakis was very happy with the service and the food. He says he'll be back for his daughter's first communion. Several of his friends talked to me about possibly renting the banquet room in the near future." Enthusiasm fed on itself. They were overdue for a spate of good luck. "Maybe we're back on our way up again, Theo."

She certainly hoped so. The due date on that loan refused to go away, and it was getting closer. She was still fifteen thousand dollars shy. It might as well have been a hundred and fifteen thousand.

Theo took her news in stride. "That is good, but that was not my question."

She stared at him. What was he talking about? "Yes, it was."

"Demetria." One tufted brow rose in a fuzzy black-and-gray arch over an eye that was as dark as midnight as he studied her face. "You know I was talking about the man you were kissing last night."

The meat mixture oozed out of the grape leaves as she squeezed them too hard. Swallowing an oath she knew Theo would have no use for, she protested vehemently. "I was not kissing him."

Foregoing his coffee for the moment, Theo drew a

stool up to the counter and sat down beside his granddaughter. "Demetria, I am not blind."

She gritted her teeth together. "Not blind, just wrong. *He* was kissing *me*."

Theo cocked his head, trying to understand why she was objecting to what he said when she was saying the same thing. "And that is a difference?"

She dropped the knife on the cutting board. "Yes, most definitely."

He didn't see it. With a voice steeped in patience, he pointed it out to her reasonably. "If you put your left foot down first when you get out of bed, or your right foot, you still end up standing and out of bed, do you not?"

She didn't care for the analogy. Maybe the subject was a little too close to home. If Theo hadn't walked in on them when he had, there was no telling where they would have wound up. Maybe even in bed, although she'd like to think that she would have put a stop to it before it went that far. Still, when Jared wasn't talking, he had the most persuasive mouth she'd even encountered.

"This is a little more complex than getting out of bed, Theo."

The knowing smile on her grandfather's lips only widened. "Yes, I know."

She could see that reasoning with him was hopeless. He was a lot like her mother when he wanted to be. The thought suddenly chilled her. "You didn't tell Ma, did you?"

Theo took umbrage that she should think such a thing of him. One hand dramatically covered his offended heart. "Tell her what? That I see you kissing a nice-looking man in our banquet room, standing so close to him that you are in his back pocket?" Demi winced at the image. "That is just between you and me." And then he laughed. "And him, of course."

She knew she was going to need an ally in this, and her grandfather was the likely choice. Hard on his own son, he'd always had a weak spot for her. "Theo, he's just trying to get to me."

The protest made him laugh even more. "I think he has stopped trying. I think he has succeeded." With the discerning taste of a hard taskmaster, Theo took a small bite of one of the dolmathes she was fashioning. He nodded his approval.

Demi felt relieved. At least this had gone right. "Maybe, in a way," she allowed, admitting to Theo what she would rather be boiled in oil than admit to anyone else. "But in no way does that mean that the restaurant is in danger of changing hands." She turned on the stool to face him. "I know what this place means to you. To the family."

He was looking at her without commenting, as if he were waiting for the right words. She knew what he wanted.

"To me." There was no question of her loyalty, but she knew that, like a man in a long-standing marriage who had once been a young groom, occasionally he needed to hear the words. Demi willingly obliged.

"I love this place and I don't intend for it to be taken over by anyone who isn't part of the family."

He believed her, but it didn't hurt to ask. "And that includes a man who makes you sigh?"

Him most of all. "And that includes a man who makes me sigh."

Slipping off the stool, Theo gave her a quick, one-armed bearlike hug and kissed the top of her head. "I knew I was right when I told your father to let you run Aphrodite." He looked around, taking a deep breath, as if his nose could tell him better than his eyes could. "So, is the coffee ready?"

Demi got off her stool, ushering him back on his. "Sit down, I'll get you a cup."

"Make it a big one," he instructed as she walked to the urn. "None of those little cups your grandmother always liked to use." Thimbles with decorations painted on them, that was all demitasse was in his opinion.

As if she hadn't heard his preference a thousand times before. "No problem, Theo."

But there was a problem, she thought, pouring the thick, black liquid. A very big problem. And it was over six feet tall, with the most sensuous lips she'd ever had the fortuitous misfortune to kiss.

She pressed her lips together and told herself that after scrubbing them half a dozen times, there was no way she could possibly still taste him.

But she did.

* * *

"But why can't I go with you, Daddy?"

Theresa had been following him around ever since he'd gotten up this morning. Dressed in dark blue overalls that brought out her fair complexion and blond hair even more than usual, she had the sticking power of industrial flypaper. He couldn't shake her loose.

Not that he wanted to, inside the house. But he wasn't going to remain inside the house for much longer this morning.

Periodically, his daughter went through clingy moods. Though she'd earned the right, it was something he was hoping she'd outgrow eventually.

Yeah, and then he'd miss it, he thought, laughing at himself.

But right now it was making things difficult. He nodded at his housekeeper, a woman he had hired specifically because of her child-care references. "Because little girls don't go to work with their daddies, Theresa. That's why you can't come with me."

Theresa pouted as she followed him into the living room. "Allison does."

Looking around, he located his briefcase. He'd meant to do work last night, but when he finally came home, he'd been far too tired to do anything but park the briefcase and go to bed.

Taking it off the hideaway desk, Jared turned his attention back to Theresa. The five-year-old was the center of his universe. It was for her that he worked so hard. So that Theresa would never lack for anything as long as she lived.

He thought of the little girl she was talking about. Allison's father was a friend of his and, like him, had sole custody of his daughter.

"Her dad's got a day-care center in his building. Besides..." he pointed out, talking to her the way he would an adult, "he stays in one office all day. I don't." Theresa knew that. He'd explained it to her when she'd asked him recently what he did all day away from her. "Don't you like staying here with Alma?"

Theresa looked over her shoulder toward the kitchen. "She's nice." She turned a sunny face up to him. "But I'd rather be with you."

She knew how to reel him in. Theresa was a con artist, he thought affectionately. But then he saw something else in her eyes. Something that looked like fear. The thought that she was afraid sliced him in two.

Kneeling, Jared got down to her level. "Honey, are you afraid I won't come back? Is that the problem?"

Her small shoulders rose and fell as she sighed. "Maybe."

Jared silently cursed his ex-wife and the cavalier attitude that had allowed her to just walk out on Theresa. In going to find herself, Gloria had abandoned the most worthwhile person in her world—her own daughter. He could have strangled her for it.

Jared smoothed back her hair from her face. "I come back every night, don't I?"

It was true, but so had Mommy. Until one day. Theresa pressed her lips together. Daddy didn't like her to cry. It made him feel bad. "Yes, but maybe sometime you won't. Like Mommy didn't."

"Sweetheart, that is never, never going to happen." Taking her hand, he drew her over to the sofa. "Come here."

Sitting down, he placed her on his lap. She weighed almost nothing. How could something so small hold his heart so fast?

"You're my best girl, Theresa." He tilted her chin up with the crook of his finger, coaxing a smile from her. "A guy always comes home to his best girl. It's in the rules."

Her eyes widened. "It is?"

He nodded solemnly. "Absolutely. I love you more than anything, Theresa," he said seriously, wishing there was some way to convince her. To make her feel instantly secure. But it was just going to take time. "Everything else can change. The sun might not come up in the morning, but I will always, always come home to you for as long as you want me to."

She studied him intently. "Forever?"

He tried not to smile. "Sounds like a plan to me."

"Okay, I guess you can go, then." She wiggled off his lap.

Jared did smile then, giving her a quick hug. "Mr. Winfield will be very happy to hear that."

Her hand in his, Theresa went with him to the front door. "If you're not going to the office, where are you going?"

He thought of Demi. When his pulse quickened, it caught him off guard. Enough hours had passed to diminish his reaction to her. Hadn't they? "Well, I am going there first, but then I'm going to go to a restaurant."

Theresa looked at him hopefully. "To eat?"

To try to form some sort of strategy. "Among other things."

Laying groundwork, even though she had no idea it was called that, Theresa asked, "Do they have games there, like Bingoland?"

"No, no games." Jared remembered the two grizzled old men hunched over their dusty chess board. "Well, there is one there, but it's just a board game."

Theresa thought of the tall stack of boxes in her room. "I like board games."

How well he knew that. The last time she'd been sick, he'd played a grand total of fifty-three games of something called "Sticky-Poo comes to Town." He'd wanted to burn the game after she'd gotten well. "This is chess, honey. Two old men are playing chess in a corner booth."

Her light eyebrows drew together in tight concentration. "What's chess?"

"Something I have to teach you someday when I have more time." Who knew? She had an affinity for games. Maybe she'd catch on quickly. He had as a kid, and she was more his than she had ever been Gloria's.

Theresa began shifting excitedly from foot to foot. "When will that be, Daddy? When will you have more time for me?"

Funny how guilt was usually served thick so that you could spread it with a knife, then use the same knife to stick into the heart of the person covered with it. Like him, he thought.

Inspiration came. No reason why he couldn't combine business with pleasure.

You already did, last night, he reminded himself.

"I tell you what, you tell Alma to get you ready and I'll come back for you around eleven. I'll bring you to the restaurant so you can see it for yourself." He grinned, knowing the idea would make her feel very grown-up. "We'll have lunch."

Theresa's eyes became huge. "Just you and me?"

"Just you and me." He skimmed her nose with his fingertip. "Eat your heart out, Allison Cooper, right?"

Theresa bobbed her head up and down. "Right!"

"Waiting for him?" Antoinette dusted her hands off as she walked over to her daughter.

Demi looked up from the stack of menus she had just cleaned. "What?"

"I have been watching you. You keep looking at the door." Antoinette nodded toward it. "I was wondering if perhaps you are waiting for him." When

Demi said nothing, she added. "The good-looking one." Still nothing. Antoinette sighed. How had she gotten such stubborn children? "The one who knows how to be a waiter. Pantella."

"Panetta," Demi corrected, annoyed. She went back to stacking menus. This was Friday, one of their better days. People liked to splurge a little on paydays.

Antoinette took the correction as an admission. "So you are waiting for him."

Leave it to her mother to make a giant leap where none was called for. She was almost too weary to be annoyed.

"No, I'm not. I'm just afraid he'll show up." And she was. After last night, she really didn't want to see Jared again for at least a few years. Maybe a century.

Antoinette wasn't buying. "You can lie to yourself, but do not try to lie to me. I am your mother. I can see things."

Damn it, why didn't everyone just leave her alone? She put her mother at the top of the list, then reminded herself that there wouldn't be a list if it wasn't for that swaggering corporate hit man.

"Lately, everyone is suffering from vision problems." Placing menus on the hostess table with a loud *thwack,* Demi walked away. She needed to do more cooking. "There is nothing to see."

Antoinette was quick to pick up on the slip. "Everyone? Who is everyone?" She glanced around the modestly filled restaurant, her eyes nming suspiciously over Theo and his friend. "Someone has seen something and you are not telling me?"

Demi stopped walking. She hung her head, knowing she was going to lose no matter which way she turned. "No, Ma, no one has seen anything. I just meant—"

Facing the front, Antoinette saw the door opening. The satisfied look was immediate. "He's here. Your patience has been rewarded. Oh, and look, he has brought his daughter."

Demi turned, her heart sinking even as her anticipation quickened.

Terrific, she thought darkly. He brought reinforcements. Just what she needed.

6

She watched them enter, the tall, dark-haired pain-in-her-side and the delicate little blond-haired girl with him. They looked as if they belonged in a Father's Day greeting card commercial.

Frustrated, Demi bit her lip. Panetta was playing dirty and he knew it. He knew there was no way she could throw him out or even tell him to leave, not when he had his daughter with him. She wouldn't do that, not to him but to the little girl.

The manipulative rat.

"Go wait on him," Demi told her mother. Suddenly acting incredibly busy, Demi began to move away from the hostess desk.

She was going to get started on tonight's desserts, Demi decided impulsively. Maybe even tomorrow's. Never mind that it was George's job and she had other things to do. She needed to get flour on her cheeks and her fingers so sticky with honey, she'd forget all about who was sitting out front. And if she got lucky, by the time she was finished, Jared would be gone.

She wasn't feeling very lucky.

Antoinette caught her daughter by the wrist before Demi had the chance to make good her escape.

"Me?" Astonishment highlighted the jovial, round face. "I have not waited on a table for ten years."

Demi tugged lightly, expecting her mother to release her. She didn't.

"It's like bicycle riding." She tugged a little harder, but her wrist remained held fast. Her mother seemed determined to keep her there. "You never forget," Demi assured her through clenched teeth.

"I never rode on a bicycle," Antoinette reminded her daughter. Then she silently indicated the duo coming toward them. "Do I have to embarrass you by pushing you toward him?" she asked in a raspy whisper.

This time, the tug was quick and hard. And successful. Freed, Demi rubbed her wrist. "You've already done both, Ma. You're way ahead of the game."

Her mother took a step to the side, not to move out of the way but to conveniently block off her avenue of retreat.

Panetta wasn't the only one into manipulation.

Bracing herself, Demi picked up the top two menus just as Jared and his daughter reached the desk.

Demi didn't even look at Jared. It was safer that way. She wasn't sure just what he'd see in her eyes if she did look at him. Probably too much.

She could get through this, Demi told herself, if

she just concentrated on the little girl and nothing else. Her smile was warm when she looked down at her. Jared's daughter looked a little like Addie, one of Guy's twins, except a lot more delicate. Like a china doll that had come to life.

"Welcome to Aphrodite," Demi said with a formal little bow. She was amused when Theresa returned it. "Is this your first time here?"

Pleased at being addressed like a grown-up, Theresa nodded solemnly. "Yes, it is."

"Well, then, we'll all be on our best behavior for you." Demi shot Jared a quick, warning look. "Won't we?"

She was putting him on notice, Jared thought, as if he were the one who was given to fits of temper. How could one woman be so damn annoying and yet so damn appealing all at the same time?

It wasn't a question about to be answered anytime soon.

Taking that into account, he was grateful to Demi for not bringing what she considered their differences into the arena while his daughter was with him. In a way, if he were being honest with himself, he supposed he'd been counting on that. If she tabled their differences and treated him civilly because of Theresa, out of necessity Demi would have to get comfortable with him. It stood to reason that if she pretended to be civil, eventually she would be, and the pretense would become the reality. After that, could appealing to her common sense be far behind?

Jared had learned a long time ago to leave little to chance. Everything was calculated toward making the inevitable negotiations between them run that much smoother. And the negotiations *were* inevitable as far as he was concerned. Under no circumstances did he intend to take no for an answer from her. To that end, he intended to turn up at the restaurant day in, day out, friendly as all hell while he integrated himself into the fabric of the lives of both the people who worked here and those who frequented the restaurant.

Into *her* life.

Jared intended to keep showing up until he was considered one of the regulars himself.

Until she trusted him.

It was part of his standard game plan. The more familiar the opposition became with him, the more likely they were going to feel that what he was saying was in their best interest.

Which, in this case, Jared firmly believed it was. Why would a woman want to be stuck working from morning until night, continually wrestling with accounts and tallies that refused to jibe, when she could just as easily be out enjoying herself? Living life instead of letting it pass her by.

He was all too familiar with the work ethic that drove her. It was that kind of overpowering ethic, that kind of drive that had killed his father.

And hers, if what he'd read in the file Winfield's investigator had put together on her was accurate. Granted that Nick Tripopulous had retired first, turning the business over to her, but he'd died of a heart attack not that long afterward. His body, worn-out by years of exhaustive work, had refused to rally even when he slowed down. It had been too late.

It wasn't the kind of fate he figured that Demi would willingly want for herself if she had an alternative. He and Jack Winfield were offering her one. In the amount of time it took to sign the papers and transfer the funds, she could be a very wealthy woman.

It was for damn sure that she wouldn't become wealthy stuck in this day-to-day rut she was in now. To Jared, the choice was simple.

All Demi had to do was stop being stubborn and take it.

She wasn't Barbara Stanwyck, for heaven's sake, trying to fight off the greedy cattle baron and keep him from seizing her land and the water rights to the valley. And he wasn't the cattle baron's henchman. The sooner she stopped acting that way, the faster this deal would go through.

And the sooner he could move on to the next project and stop fantasizing about what could have been last night if they hadn't been interrupted. Thinking along those lines wasn't going to do either one of them any good.

So why couldn't he stop?

"Will this table do?" Demi stopped beside a table that was in the center of the restaurant. The one she'd offered Jared when he had walked in the first time.

Rather than look up at her father for confirmation, Theresa nibbled on her lower lip, appearing to think the question over herself. An independent, Demi thought, getting a kick out of the child. An independent just like she had been when she was Theresa's age.

"Or would you rather sit over here?" Demi pointed to the next-to-the-last booth against the wall.

Theresa turned and saw Theo and Alex for the first time. Her small mouth formed a perfectly round circle. "Oh." And then she beamed as she looked up at Demi. "The chest game."

"Chess, honey," Jared corrected.

Theresa took the correction in stride. "That's right, chess."

But Demi didn't take in stride the fact that Theresa knew about the chess game. She looked at Jared sharply. "You told her about the game?"

What had he done, coached his daughter about the restaurant he was trying to take over? Was he actually using his own daughter as a pawn to try to lull Demi into a complacent state? Didn't this man have any sort of a conscience or scruples at all?

One look at Demi's face told him what she was thinking. He wanted to deny it, but there was no way he could get into that now. With Demi involved, it would escalate into angry words in a matter of minutes, and he wasn't about to subject Theresa to any more ugliness if he could possibly help it. She'd already been through enough in her young life.

"It came up in the conversation," he said mildly. "She was talking about games. I told her about this one." He rested his hand on his daughter's shoulder. "Theresa loves games."

Her suspicions were not put to rest, despite the affection in his voice as he said his daughter's name. "Is that true?" Demi's eyes held Theresa's. "Do you like games, Theresa?"

"I love games." The passion in Theresa's voice was not the kind that could be rehearsed. Not unless she was this generation's answer to Shirley Temple. "All kinds of games."

Demi nodded, purposely avoiding looking at Jared. "Well, then, I guess we'll let you peek in on this one."

Very deliberately she took Theresa's hand in hers. Leaving Jared to follow if he chose, she took the little girl over to her grandfather's table.

Though he heard them approach, Theo didn't look up. It was all part of the mystique. He liked to appear as if he was so engrossed in the strategies of the game before him that he was oblivious to everything else that was going on around him.

Demi knew better. Nothing went on around him that Theo didn't notice.

"Are we bothering them?" Theresa asked her in a small whisper.

Demi grinned, won over without a single shot. Panetta didn't deserve a little girl as sweet as this.

"Don't worry, an earthquake wouldn't bother them," she assured Theresa.

At that, Theo did raise his eyes from the board. His perpetual opponent had already turned around in his seat to get a better look at the pint-size audience they'd attracted.

"And who is this you have brought?" Theo asked.

Theresa raised her small chin proudly as she put out her hand to the old man. "My name is Theresa Panetta. How do you do?"

Amused and tickled, Theo took the offered hand. It was swallowed up completely within his large paw.

"I do very well, Theresa Panetta. I am Theo." He pointed to himself with the tip of his pipe, then indicated the man sitting opposite him. "This sorry-looking man who is pretending he understands the game we are playing is Alex."

Affronted, Alex protested heatedly. "I do understand." He nodded a silent greeting to Theresa.

Theo dismissed him with a wave of the same pipe. "Do not listen to him. That is only his pride talking, not his knowledge. He has no knowledge." He snorted when Alex began to bluster. It was a familiar game for all concerned, as familiar as the one on the table. Theo looked at Theresa confidently. "In thirty minutes, I could teach you how to play better than he does."

Next to being with her father, Theresa liked nothing better than learning a new game. Her eyes danced with excitement. "Would you really teach me? Would you teach me now?"

Demi watched Theo's reaction with interest. The little girl had managed to capture Theo in the palm of her hand with no effort at all.

Jared placed a subduing hand on Theresa's shoulder, moving her back from the table. "Theresa, don't bother them now, honey. These men are busy with their game."

But Theo waved away Jared's words. He nodded at his friend of over fifty years. "He is busy, trying to think. As you can see, it is taking all his energy. Me, I am just busy trying not to fall asleep." He moved the half-empty drink in front of him to the next spot, then moved himself as well. Relocated, he patted the newly vacated space beside him. "Come. You want to learn? I teach you."

Alex scowled at Theo. "But we are in the middle of playing."

The protest had no effect. Theo was already looking forward to having an eager pupil. "With you, I can teach and play at the same time."

Theresa looked up at Jared hopefully.

This was going better than he could possibly have foreseen. Jared nodded. "If it's really all right with them, it's all right with me."

Theresa clapped her hands together gleefully, securing three sets of hearts for her trophy case. Jared doubted that a day went by when he didn't fall in love with her all over again, just the way he had the first time he laid eyes on her. It made his heart glad to know that there were others who appreciated the little girl just as much as he did.

"Fine. It is settled. I teach you chess." Theo glanced toward Jared, who was still standing there. He waved him off. "You can go about your business." The dark eyes alighted on Demi before he focused his attention on the little girl sitting beside him. His meaning was clear. "Now, first," he began, "I will tell you the names of the pieces...."

Demi knew when she'd been dismissed. There was nothing left to do but take Jared back to his table. This could take quite a while. Once Theo got started teaching the fine points of the game, there was no stopping him.

"She has lovely manners," Demi commented. She placed the menus on the table, then looked at Jared. "Who taught her?"

He should have known this would happen. With Theresa out of the way, the boxing gloves had come on. "I did. Is that so hard to believe?"

Demi saw no reason to waste her breath being polite. "Yes."

She didn't mean that, he thought. It was something she felt she had to say, to redraw the lines that had been blurred. But he didn't want to give her the chance to etch them in again. "I thought maybe after last night, we were on a slightly better footing."

"Think again." Then, though she knew she was making an error, she had to ask, "Is that how you operate when you find yourself not getting what you want? You seduce the opponent?''

He laughed shortly. He saw that she took offense and he quickly let her in on the joke.

"The last half-dozen people I've dealt with were all men." The smile softened as he let his eyes drift over her. The quick, urgent surge was one he didn't welcome or feel prepared to meet. It took him prisoner anyway. "And you're not my opponent."

"No? We're on opposite sides of this. What does that make us?" She wished he wouldn't look at her that way—as if she were a desirable woman. She couldn't keep her mind on thinking of him as morally reprehensible if he looked at her like that.

He watched her mouth move, and thought of last night. Desire came of its own accord, bringing luggage. "Offhand, I'd say attracted to each other."

Because she was sinking, Demi began to think of the long process involved in making baklava. It was the only thing that saved her. "Offhand or on, I'd say that you'd say anything to get what you wanted."

"No," Jared answered. He could see she didn't believe him. "That's a blanket 'no,'" he elaborated. "I do not say whatever is expedient, not in my professional life—"

"And in your private life?" she pressed, although she knew that this couldn't be considered private. Whatever he did was all centered around his job, no matter what he said to the contrary. But for now, because it stimulated her, she played the game.

"I don't really have a private life," he told her honestly. "You just met what there is of it." He gestured toward the last booth and his daughter.

And he expected her to swallow that? A man who looked the way he did, with a face that was the kind women dreamed about? She almost laughed in it.

"And you're a practicing monk?"

He didn't know whether to be flattered by her tone or annoyed. Since he was here on business, he chose middle ground. He also, for reasons of simplicity he supposed, chose to be honest with her.

"I'm not practicing, Demi." He slowly ran his fingers along the stem of the water glass the busboy had brought to the table. "I've got it pretty much down pat by now. The nature of my work doesn't leave much time for a private life. Whatever time I do have, I spend with Theresa. Dating is something I just don't make room for in my life."

Demi realized that she was staring at the way he was stroking the glass. Staring and reacting. Why else would she suddenly feel as if the heat had been turned on in the room?

She was becoming her own worst enemy in this.

"And why is that?" she asked with effort.

He surprised himself by telling her. It wasn't something he generally talked about. "Ever hear the old saying about once burnt, twice wary? I was burnt once, Demi. Third-degree."

She tried not to let the pain she heard in his voice affect her. But she could feel herself being drawn in despite herself. She'd always been a sucker for a hard-luck story, she thought. Even if the hard luck belonged to a manipulative snake.

"Theresa's mother?"

He nodded. He'd gotten over her a long time ago, but not over the pain she'd left in her wake. The scars were there to remind him. "It's not an experience that makes me want to contemplate grabbing another red-hot handle again anytime soon...."

She could understand that. But what she couldn't understand was what had happened between them after the banquet. "Then last night was calculated."

It would seem that way to an outsider, he supposed. While his job—his career—was important to him, seduction was not an option. For him that would be going more than the allowed amount of steps beyond persuasion.

"Not calculated," he corrected. "Just something nice...very nice."

"You expect me to believe that?"

"I expect you to know the difference between a lie and the truth."

That was just the trouble. She didn't know the difference, not in his case. What she wanted to be the truth could very well be the lie.

Every shred of common sense she had told her she was crazy, yet she really wanted to believe him. Maybe she was spending too much time beside a hot oven, she thought. It had obviously vaporized the part of her brain where common sense took refuge.

Demi heard her grandfather laughing as he coaxed Theresa to make a move on the board. Demi retreated to a safer subject than the one they were debating. "Why did you bring her here?"

She was on the defensive again. He heard the challenge in her voice. "Because she asked to come."

The tender feelings that had been forming vanished. Another insult to her intelligence. Did he actually expect her to believe that?

"Oh, she said, 'Take me to Aphrodite.'" Sarcasm dripped from her voice.

"No. She asked to come with me to work. Said she wanted to be with me. Since I was coming here after I checked in, I didn't see the harm in it."

All right, she'd give him the benefit of the doubt on that one. But that still didn't change the bottom line between them.

"And why are you still coming here after I said no? How many times do I have to tell you that Aphrodite is not for sale? Not to you, not to anyone." Frustrated, she demanded in a voice that was controlled only insofar as she didn't want Theresa to suffer the ignoble pain of hearing someone yell at her father, "Do I need to get a dog to get you to leave me alone? Or a bouncer?"

"I don't want to bother you, Demi," he told her simply. "I came back to Aphrodite for the same reason most of your patrons return. The food. The atmosphere." He leaned back in his chair, his eyes on hers. "I wanted to introduce Theresa to something a little more sophisticated and tasteful than Bingoland.'' He paused, and then grinned engagingly. "Thanks for curbing that temper of yours around her."

She knew of several women in her acquaintance who would have killed to be the recipient of the grin he was aiming her way. But she wasn't one of them. And she didn't want him getting any wrong ideas as to why she was being civil to him.

"That wasn't for you, that was for her." She glanced back at Theresa. Her head was bowed, inclined toward Theo's. It brought back warm memories. She'd sat like that with him more than twenty years ago while Theo had taught her the finer points of the game. "Why should she get caught in the cross fire?"

"No cross fire, Demi," he promised her. "I'm here strictly as a patron, nothing more." And that was the way it was going to be until she trusted him. Until she saw him not as the enemy, but as a friend. Someone who could offer her a better life.

But there was more, Demi thought, trying not to let herself be carried away. There was a lot more. And not just because he represented Winfield, Inc. Jared Panetta represented the first stirrings she'd felt since...

She'd never felt stirrings like that, Demi realized. Having a social life had never been a high priority on her crowded agenda. She'd been too dedicated to the family business to think about dating and wrestling with boys whose hormones had gone into overdrive.

Even if she had, the men in her family would have scared away any potential applicant for the position just by the nature of their very existence. She smiled to herself. The wall formed by the combined forces of her father, her brother and her grandfather had not been one that was easily scaled. And none had tried.

She eyed Jared skeptically, although maybe, just maybe, there was a little room to be won over. "So, you've given up the idea of getting me to sell to Winfield?"

To say yes would have been to arouse her suspicions further. He played it honestly. "For the time being. Let's just say it's on the back burner."

It was an analogy she could readily appreciate. "Things on the back burner have a habit of being forgotten and getting burned."

He shrugged as if that really didn't concern him at the moment. "Right now I would really like to sample that dish I was serving to everyone at the party last night. Is there any left over?"

He'd cleared away a number of servings of the individual lamb pies. People had been too full to eat any more. But she might have resurrected what was left into a subsequent meal that was on today's menu, bearing some resemblance to its former state.

Food was something they could talk about with relative safety. "As a matter of fact, there is. I'll bring you some."

Turning, she hurried to the kitchen. It was as good as any excuse to retreat.

7

"We're back," Theresa announced with glee as she hurried to Theo's booth.

After nearly a week of coming here every afternoon with her father, Theresa no longer felt she had to hang back on ceremony the way she'd been taught. It wasn't as if she were going to one of those places where she had to be on her very best, special behavior. Thriving in the warm atmosphere, Theresa had made herself at home at Aphrodite.

Jared smiled to himself as he watched his daughter run across the room. He was beginning to really see what the attraction was. He found himself looking forward to coming here, too, if only to watch Theresa.

And perhaps to see Demi again.

No reason why he couldn't enjoy himself as he was laying his groundwork, he reasoned.

Theo had looked up when he heard Theresa's announcement. The smile on his face was broad as he welcomed the sight of the little girl rushing toward him. Though he remained seated, he caught her in a quick, one-armed bear hug.

116 THE OFFER SHE COULDN'T REFUSE

"Ah, I knew there was a reason Alex began shaking in his shoes." He nodded sagely, his eyes bright with pleasure. "Ready for another lesson, little one?"

Theresa nodded vigorously. She was already scooting up on her knees in the seat.

"All she talks about at night is you and this game and the restaurant," Jared told Theo as he approached the booth.

That much was true. Theresa had no grandfather to call her own. She was too young to remember his father, and Gloria's father had died years ago. Jared had little doubt that Theresa had drafted Theo to be her surrogate grandfather.

"So, you could not wait to be here, eh, little one? As it should be." Theo ran his wide hand over the little girl's head.

The gesture was surprisingly gentle. Jared could easily picture that same hand delivering a punch that would send an opponent crashing to the ground. The man might be short in stature, but even at his age, he looked as strong as a bull in his prime.

"Everyone who comes here wants to become part of our little family," Theo confided to her.

Theresa's eyes were huge. "Can I be part of your family, too?"

Jared heard the eagerness, the hunger in her voice. It was worse than he'd thought. With Gloria out of Theresa's life and his brother and sister living in different cities, he was the only family that his daughter had. It wasn't just a matter of thinking of Theo as her surrogate grandfather; she was lonely for a family. He hadn't known, until this moment, just how lonely she was, or how much she wanted to feel a part of something.

Guilt, never far from the scene these days, rose its head to take another bite out of him with its sharp teeth. Guilt at having been oblivious to Theresa's feeling this way. Guilt at orchestrating something so temporary that affected her so much. This would all disappear from Theresa's life shortly. Winfield allowed his restaurants a free hand, but only up to a point. Once Aphrodite was sold, there would be no need, or time for that matter, for Jared to continue coming here. And Theo and his friend wouldn't be at the last booth playing "chest" any longer. That, too, would have to stop.

How was that going to affect Theresa?

"But of course," Theo was saying to Theresa. "You can be my official great-granddaughter. Now come," he coaxed, nodding at the board, "let us show this old man he is no match for us."

"Tomorrow, I will bring *my* great-grandson," Alex grumbled. He appeared to settle in for a showdown that was never really going to materialize. Neither man doubted that the game, in one form or another, was destined to go on forever.

Theo laughed. The loud, booming sound drew several pairs of eyes their way. Theresa looked pleased at being at the center of attention.

"It is a deal," Theo told Alex. "But it still will

not help you." He looked at the child by his elbow. "You will come tomorrow?"

"Yes." The declaration burst out of her mouth. Realizing she couldn't agree without her father's permission, Theresa looked at Jared.

How could he say no, even if he wanted to? The look in her eyes completely undid him. Jared nodded.

Funny how things were turning out. He'd originally brought Theresa with him to spend a little time with her, but also with any eye out to impress Demi because he knew how much family meant to her. He'd wanted to come across to Demi as someone more than just the man representing the company that wanted to take over her restaurant. He wanted her to see him as a human being.

Now, instead of winning her over to his side, the reverse seemed to be happening. He was being drawn over to Demi's side. Downright charmed by her side. It was easy to see why Winfield wanted this place despite its present cash-flow problem.

The money problem could easily be solved. It was in part self-made. If Demi just didn't carry so many people on the books, this place could become a gold mine.

God, he was beginning to sound more like Winfield every day, Jared thought. He didn't know if that was a good thing or not. He would have once. Would have felt that it was a good thing and been proud of it. Now he just wasn't sure.

Theo, his hand hovering over Theresa's as she

made her decision and picked up the queen, raised his eyes expectantly to Jared's face. "Well, why are you still here? She is in the office."

He was being rather bluntly dismissed. Jared didn't mind. He was only getting in the way here, he thought. "Thanks. Don't make any trouble," he told Theresa fondly.

Theo laughed again. "Making trouble, that is for Demetria to do," he called after Jared.

Amen to that. Demi certainly meant trouble when it came to him.

He didn't want to get tangled up with her, Jared thought. Especially not emotionally. He worked best when only appearing to be the personification of friendliness while managing to reserve a small piece of himself, keeping it on hold. He couldn't seem to do that here.

Usually, he came, made a good offer, waited until all systems were smooth and running, and then left, always proceeding on to the next deal that was to be made, the next restaurant that Winfield had set his sights on acquiring. He remembered all the acquisitions in detail, but they were the sort of details that could be found on a ledger.

Not the kind that existed in the heart. Certainly not the kind that could take his breath away and make him daydream at the oddest times.

Like now.

She was alone in the office.

Jared leaned his shoulder against the doorjamb and

just watched her quietly for a moment, enjoying the fact that she seemed oblivious to his presence. Even watching her chew the top of a pencil, lost in thought, made his pulse quicken. It wasn't a good sign.

She sensed him before she even looked up from her accounting book.

It was the scent of the cologne that gave him away. This time, she knew she wasn't imagining it, as she had last night, wrestling with her pillow and the sleeplessness that refused to give her any peace. It was far too strong, far too lethal to just be her imagination.

"So, you're back." *Again,* she thought. Demi closed her book firmly as she turned the chair to face the doorway.

Jared noted the way she kept her hand over the book. She still saw him as the enemy, he thought. And maybe he was.

What bothered him was that for reasons that were apart from his job, he didn't want to be.

He nodded in response. "Theresa wanted another lesson."

"And you dropped everything to bring her."

Her mouth mocked him, but he felt himself getting lost in it anyway, remembering the feel, the texture, the taste of her lips pressed against his.

"Very selfless of you," she concluded.

Not waiting for an invitation, Jared came in. He leaned a hip against the edge of the desk and looked at her. She looked tired, he thought. And more tempting every time he saw her. He didn't know what to do about that.

"Not entirely," he allowed. "*I* wanted to come back, too."

He was good, she thought. He knew just how to add enough honesty to make himself sound believable and aboveboard. "For another crack at wearing me down?"

Back to thrusting and parrying, he thought, amused. Jared spread his hands wide. "For another serving of dessert, another helping of scintillating conversation." He shrugged, nodding toward the kitchen and what was beyond. "It's like you said, this place really does grow on you."

She believed he meant that. Demi studied him in silence.

Maybe that was something she could work with, she thought, her enthusiasm building at a surprising rate. If he kept showing up on her doorstep like this, she could turn the tables on him, show him just how special this place was to everyone, especially her.

If she really thought about it, Jared wasn't an extension of the monster she saw herself fighting. He wasn't Jack Winfield. He was different. Jared had proven that to her by the way he behaved toward his daughter.

They'd been coming here for almost a week and by now, the act would have worn a little thin if it *were* an act. But it was clear to her that Jared put being a father very high on his busy list of things to do. That put him one up on her own father and humanized him in her eyes.

That, and the kiss they'd shared that night.

"Yes, it does grow on you." She looked at him pointedly. "Which is why I'm never letting it go."

"Keeper of the flame, eh?" His smile teased her. Before she had a chance to retort, he nodded at the book beneath her hand. "You still do the books by hand?" In this technically oriented age when computers were dialing phones for people, he found that almost impossible to believe. And yet, somehow it fit.

Before answering, Demi opened the side drawer and dropped the ledger in. Very deliberately she closed the drawer again and then locked it.

"Yes." Her eyes held his, a defiant light rising in them again.

He didn't feel like going a few rounds with her. For a while at least, he wanted to see what it felt like to be on the same side and just steep his senses in her. It didn't look as if that was going to happen just yet.

"Still don't trust me, do you?"

He had no idea how often she caught herself wishing that she could. Deep in the recesses of the night, as she lay awake thinking about him, entertaining impossible thoughts.

But she had never been a fool and she wasn't going to start being one now. "Should I?"

Jared shrugged. Maybe he wouldn't trust him, either, in her place.

But he wasn't the enemy and he didn't want her to think of him that way. Still, proclaiming as much would only accomplish the reverse, and he knew it. Jared curbed his impatience, an impatience that surprised him by its very existence.

He took the conversation on a slightly different track. "Why don't you use a computer?"

That was simple enough to answer. "Because there's no money for things like that. I use it only for the very essentials. Hardware in our case refers to a new pot, not a new monitor." She rose and pushed her chair against the desk. "Every penny we make goes back into the business." Maybe that was the way out. "Why don't you tell Winfield that this is not a money-making restaurant and he's just wasting his time and yours by looking into it?"

It was true. You had to love Aphrodite to put in the amount of time required to run it. Men like Winfield didn't love places, they loved profit. Which made his interest in it a mystery to her.

"Just why does he want this place, anyway?" she asked Jared.

Was it his imagination, or was the room getting a little smaller, a little more crammed as he stood here beside her? It certainly felt that way to him. He supposed it meant that hormones could be held in abeyance for only so long before they took on a life of their own.

He tried to concentrate on her question. It was a logical one, in light of her situation. "It has a great location, an excellent reputation and fantastic food." He could swear to the latter himself.

The location was purely happenstance. When her grandfather had chosen it, there were only a few houses in the area. The word *mall* hadn't even been added to the vocabulary yet. It was just a matter of pure luck that Aphrodite wound up on the outskirts of one of the major malls in Southern California, or the West Coast for that matter.

But as far as reputation and food went, well, that was where the work came in. She took personal pride in as well as responsibility for both.

"If Winfield could buy the restaurant, he'd certainly get the location, and some of the residue reputation would follow, but as for the food, well, a deed wouldn't entitle him to any of the recipes. Those are all family secrets and they stay within the family."

A self-satisfied smile curved her mouth, making it more tempting than he thought he could successfully resist. But he did his damnedest.

"The only way anyone gets their hands on them is by marrying into the family," she said.

He knew she meant that as the ultimate obstacle. Just for a brief moment, he didn't quite see it that way. "That doesn't seem like such a stiff price to pay."

He was just making conversation. A flip remark at best. There was no reason why her heart should suddenly constrict within her chest. None at all, damn it.

She drew a breath, then slowly let it out. It didn't help.

"I have to go help George," she muttered, her eyes refusing to leave his. "He always gets overwhelmed right about now." It was almost noon. It always got busier around noon. "He can't handle more than one course at a time."

She moved to leave. Jared didn't. He remained in her way, held fast by the look in her eyes, by her scent and by a need that was so urgent, it scared the hell out of him. "And what do you get overwhelmed by?"

Steady, Demi, he's just trying to get to you. Surprise, he was succeeding. "Pushy men who ask too many questions."

The pulse in her throat was throbbing. It urged him on. "I've got one more for you. Why didn't you ever get married?"

Who was feeding him lines—her mother? "I am. To the restaurant."

She was far too warm and vibrant to be satisfied with just that. What about her needs as a woman? "You can't take it home with you."

She laughed shortly. How many nights had she fallen asleep, her bed littered with paper pertaining to the inventory, and order forms? "You'd be surprised."

He was making her nervous. The thought excited him beyond words. "Not to bed."

The phrase whispered along her skin, making her

flesh melt. Still, she struggled to resist. "My bed is none of your business."

She didn't mean that, not really. He could see it in her eyes. "Maybe I'd like to make it my business."

He was crowding her. Without taking a step toward her, he was crowding her, cutting off her escape. Her air. Her defenses were snapping like dried matchsticks. "Just how far would you go to convince me to sell?"

His mistake was in deluding himself that he was doing this because of work. He didn't want her making the same one.

This time, he did move. Placing one hand on the doorjamb just above her head, the other by her shoulder, he framed her.

"This has nothing to do with convincing you to sell. Nothing to do with the way I earn my living, or you yours. This has everything to do with the fact that I seem to be having trouble thinking clearly ever since I walked into this place."

She swallowed, wishing she could tear her eyes away from his mouth. Wishing she could stop remembering what it had felt like against hers.

"That's not my fault." It was meant to be a loud protest. It was just the barest whisper.

"Oh, but it is." He moved his head as if to kiss her, stopping just short of her mouth. Jared absorbed the anticipation jumping around within him as if it were a life-giving force. "It is very much your fault. Theresa's crazy about this place, about you."

Demi felt as if the words she spoke were slipping between her lips in slow motion. "Theresa has good taste."

When his mouth curved, she could swear she felt it. "She gets that from me."

With one final attempt at escape, she braced her hands against his chest. But there was no strength with which to push. "You're in my way."

As it deepened, the smile on his lips curved even farther into her body. "I know."

Where was this strange rushing sound in her ears coming from? Had George left the water running again? Oh, please, let George have left the water running again. "Do I have to move you?"

He liked the way her hands fluttered along his chest, liked every damn thing about this femme fatale in shrew's clothing. He knew it was going to be his downfall. "Why don't you try?"

The rest was inevitable. Just the way she'd imagined that it would be—a hundred times since it had first happened.

Just the way she'd ached for it to happen again.

His arms slipped around her waist and he drew her closer to him. Too close for a prayer. There was no escape.

She didn't even pretend to fight it. She wanted to taste his mouth on hers so badly, she couldn't even make a show of trying to fend him off. If she did, she might succeed. And lose. Because she wanted him to kiss her more than she wanted anything else in the world.

And much more than she knew was good for her.

It was a matter of overwhelming needs taking precedence over common sense.

"You're too tall," she muttered against his mouth, rising on her toes for better contact.

The next thing she knew, there was no floor beneath her feet. With his arms tightly wrapped around her, Jared had picked her up.

Her body slid slowly, seductively up along his until her face was almost level with his.

"Better?" he asked.

She didn't know about better, but it was certainly a lot hotter.

"Almost," she whispered, her eyes touching him the way she wanted her lips to do.

Her breath tantalized him as it skimmed along his face. He could feel his body growing rigid with needs he had completely ignored since Gloria had left. Needs that he'd thought were all but gone from his life for good.

So much about living out his life as a monk.

Jared didn't remember bringing his mouth to hers. Didn't remember the mechanics of the act at all. All he was aware of was the explosion that went off in his veins. The one that detonated instantly as soon as contact was made.

Unlike the first time, this kiss was almost ruthlessly hungry.

No one was more surprised by its intensity than he was. He could feel her heart pounding wildly against him, equating the rhythm within his own chest. His own heart felt as if it would burst.

It was a hell of a way to go.

Damn it, why this woman? Why now? Nothing could come of it. The path was completely cluttered with issues and obstacles. She wouldn't believe that this was happening of its own accord and not because of the restaurant. And he couldn't blame her.

But none of that mattered now.

Nothing mattered except this wild, heady rush that overtook him when he was with her like this. He struggled to absorb it as much as he sanely could while it was happening.

There was no denying that she was driving him crazy. His hold on reality was perilously close to slipping completely out of his hands.

Suddenly, a booming voice broke the silence. "Hey, is this some new way I haven't heard of of saying no to a sales pitch?"

Jared almost dropped her. Only quick reflexes had him tightening his arms again so that she wouldn't land on her feet with an ignoble thud.

Embarrassment and annoyance joined forces with surprise and disorientation as they turned in unison toward the doorway.

Guy was grinning at them, clearly amused. Demi curbed the urge to tell him what he could do with his question. Ordinarily, she would have gladly told him. But Guy wasn't alone.

Composing herself with admirable speed, Demi had to be satisfied with shooting her brother a dirty look. She prayed she didn't sound as breathless as she felt.

"Jared, you know my brother, Guy." Amused, Guy nodded his greeting. Demi dragged her hand through her hair, silently vowing to get even with Guy first chance she got for what he was obviously thinking right now. "This is my sister-in-law, Nancy." Her tone softened. "And my three very favorite people in the whole world, A.J., Addie and the newest addition to our family." Demi gently moved the blanket away from the sleeping baby in Nancy's arms. "Antoinette."

Taking refuge with the children, Demi slipped an arm around each of the twin's shoulders. "So, what are you guys doing here?"

It was Guy who answered. "We were in the neighborhood and I couldn't talk them out of coming here. Seems our place ranks higher than Bingoland with them."

Demi looked at Guy over her shoulder. He was still wearing that amused, annoying-as-hell expression. She had an urge to hit him upside the head. Only the presence of his children saved him. And he knew it, she thought.

"Oh, so now it's 'our' place, is it? When was the

last time you put in any time behind an apron, brother dear?"

"He cooks?" Jared asked, surprised.

Guy looked far too rugged to be able to do anything but boil water. But then he thought of Theo and Demi's claim that the man cooked rings around all of them. Men did rank among the top chefs of the world. He just didn't see that rank being shared by a policeman better suited to posing for a Greek statue. This family was full of surprises.

"I insist on it," Nancy told Jared. "He's not as good as Demi or Theo," she went on playfully, "but he holds his own in the kitchen."

"She says that because she hates to cook," Guy confided.

Nancy saw no reason to deny it. "Guilty as charged."

She needed some air, Demi thought. And to get away from the questions she saw in Guy's eyes. Hell, she needed to get away from both men.

"C'mon, kids, there's someone outside I'd like you to meet," Demi told A.J. and Addie.

Swiftly transferring the baby into Guy's arms, Nancy hurried after her sister-in-law.

"I like him," she said in a voice that just barely qualified as a whisper.

Terrific, he probably heard that. Demi refused to turn around to satisfy her curiosity.

"Good, then you can have him," Demi told her with a note of finality. She wasn't up to discussing

Jared with anyone, not even with someone she numbered among her best friends. Not with all her feelings churned up in such an uproar.

"My wife's a modern woman," Guy explained to Jared, nodding at the bundle she'd just deposited in his arms.

The baby, as if realizing she was under discussion, opened her eyes. They were a bright green. Like Demi's, Jared thought.

"How old?" Jared asked Guy.

"Nine months. Nothing like holding your own in your arms." Guy's pride was hard to miss. "Just like a piece of heaven."

A feeling of wistfulness came over him as Jared remembered Theresa at this age. "May I?"

Yeah, Guy thought as he gently slipped his daughter into Jared's arms, *this one would do very nicely.*

Demi gave in and looked back, telling herself it was only to see what was taking Guy so long. She saw the look on Jared's face as he took her niece into his arms. Awed. Wistful.

It was then that she knew she was doomed.

8

"So, how's it coming along?" Jack Winfield's booming voice preceded him as the large-boned, tall businessman strode into Jared's office. His very presence commandeered the space. "Are you making any progress?"

Surprised, Jared looked up from the notes he was reviewing. Notes he had made to himself regarding Aphrodite. Winfield never knocked or bothered to make appointments with the people who worked for him, other than the regular meetings he'd scheduled for Friday mornings. He believed there was merit in catching employees unaware, while they were going through the usual routine of their jobs. Those who pleased him were well rewarded. Those who didn't were shown the door. Quickly. Stress was an integral factor in working for Winfield, and lately it was becoming more so.

Normally above it, Jared was beginning to feel the effects himself. There was a growing pain between his shoulders that sharpened at the sound of Winfield's greeting.

Jared closed the folder with his notes, dropping it on his desk as he sat up. "Jack, I thought you were in Hawaii."

"I was." Making no pretense at niceties, Winfield turned the folder around to face him and absently thumbed through the report. Jared wasn't taken in by the disinterested expression. He'd been with Winfield too long. Nothing that was remotely connected to Winfield, Inc., disinterested the man.

Winfield looked up at Jared, an empty smile twitching his mouth. "Now I'm here, ready to forge ahead." The smile disappeared as quickly as it had appeared. "Are we forging?"

Even if he were given to lying, Jared wouldn't have attempted it now. Not with Winfield. The man always knew if he was being lied to. "Not yet."

Winfield's mournfully long face remained impassive. His eyes continued to be unfathomable. "Why not?"

Was it his imagination, or was he feeling uncomfortable in Winfield's presence? If he didn't know better, he would have speculated that somehow, mysteriously, his alliances had shifted without his consciously acknowledging the fact.

Jared answered Winfield's question with the truth. Though the man was impatient, Jared had never known him to be unreasonable. Winfield understood that some negotiations needed more time than others.

"Ms. Tripopulous is still averse to the idea of selling the family business."

Singular streaks of color subtly crept up both sides of Winfield's neck, making the veins stand out.

"Well, get her *un*averse to it." It was a quiet, steely order, but the intensity took Jared by surprise. He didn't remember ever seeing Winfield this adamant about an acquisition before. "Do whatever it takes. I want that restaurant as part of my stable."

As if sensing he was coming on too strong, Winfield let out a long, cleansing breath. Since he genuinely liked Jared and had told him more than once he thought of him as his protégé, he threw an arm around the younger man's shoulders in a show of camaraderie.

"Look, Jared, I have a dream. You believe in dreams, don't you? Every man's got to have a dream. Mine's when someone says they want to eat out— whether it's home-style cooking, Italian food, Chinese, Thai, steak and lobster or Greek—they'll think of one of my restaurants. Reasonable food at reasonable prices." It was the slogan he'd started out with eighteen years ago when he'd acquired his very first restaurant. "I deliver whatever I promise." The arm slipped off Jared's shoulders. Winfield looked at him pointedly. "I expect the people I have working for me to do the same."

Jared was painfully aware of what he'd said when he took on the assignment. That he would have the contract, signed and sealed, on Winfield's desk within a week. They were well into week three.

"This is taking longer than I thought it might," he admitted.

"But you are making progress." It wasn't a question; it was a statement Winfield wanted him to verify.

Jared looked out the window. The weather outside seemed a lot better than the weather inside his office. "Yes, I'm making progress."

Of course, it all depended on your definition of progress, he added silently. His involved seeing his daughter smile. And feeling as if his own heart had been taken out of deep freeze. Unfortunately, it had little to nothing to do with what *Winfield* called progress, but there was no point in going into that just yet. Winfield's mood was threatening to turn foul at the least provocation. Jared didn't particularly want to provide it.

Winfield was studying him when Jared turned around. "Well, you're about to make progress a little faster."

"Meaning?" Jared had an uneasy feeling he wasn't going to like what he heard.

Winfield smiled with feeling for the first time since he'd walked in.

"Meaning the lady owes a note of some substance—as far as she's concerned anyway—to First Federal Pacific. A note her late father foolishly took out and one that she won't have a prayer of meeting if her suppliers suddenly decide to dry up her credit."

The self-satisfied smile widened, chilling Jared.

"She can't make meals for her patrons if she can't buy the ingredients she needs."

It took Jared a minute to assimilate what Winfield was saying. Not because he didn't understand, but because he didn't want to believe that a man he'd respected and at one time strove to emulate was capable of something so underhanded and deceitful. There had to be some explanation other than the one that stared him in the face. There was no reason to stoop to this level, other than sheer stubbornness taken to a perverse degree.

"Did you tell her suppliers to cut her off?"

Winfield's frown told Jared he didn't care for his tone. "Not yet, but I'm thinking about it. I'm thinking real hard about it." He laughed to himself. "It would make things a damn sight simpler." Though Jared was beginning to annoy him, he was very pleased with himself. "There's not much to do in Hawaii if you don't want to roast like a stuffed pig, so I started calling around, checking out a few things."

It meant that Winfield was becoming impatient with him, Jared thought. Obviously he didn't think he was moving fast enough on this deal. Why? What was the sudden hurry? It seemed to him that the more Winfield got, the more he wanted. Jared remembered the story he'd read to Theresa the other night about the escalating greed of a fisherman's wife. Apparently it didn't happen only in fairy tales.

"Seems we have a few suppliers in common," Winfield was saying. "And they sure as hell don't want to get on my bad side and lose my business. My accounts are fifteen times the size of hers."

That was because he had fifteen restaurants to her one. How could he be proud of what he was contemplating? "That's not fair, Jack."

Winfield's eyes narrowed until they looked as if they were no larger than tiny pinpricks shooting out twin laser beams of displeasure.

"Fair? Who cares about fair? That's *business*, Jared. If you're so concerned about her feelings, make that woman sell to us before things get too ugly for her. Tell her she can come work for me once the ink dries on the bill of sale."

Had Winfield changed in the last year, or had the man always been like this and Jared just hadn't realized it? Or were his freshly unearthed feelings coloring everything? "I already told her that, Jack."

"And?"

Jared supposed that one of the reasons Winfield was as successful as he was was because he refused to take no for an answer. He just couldn't bring himself to believe that people actually meant to turn him down. "And, no sale."

The bony shoulders artfully concealed beneath the expertly tailored expensive jacket lifted, then fell carelessly. "Pity. Still, it won't affect the final outcome. The lady will sell to us, Jared. It's only a matter of time. Now get going."

Jared couldn't get rid of the bitter taste in his mouth. It overwhelmed everything, refusing to be cleansed by anything he drank or the mints he kept popping into his mouth one at a time. The taste was so bitter, he could hardly bring himself to swallow.

He needed to go somewhere and clear his head so he could deal with the situation logically, facing it like so many equations spread out on a white sheet of ruled paper. Logic had always been his ally before.

His ally wasn't all that sure what to do confronted by the extraneous feelings that insisted on bouncing around within him. Feelings, and a sense of honor that refused to let him accept Winfield's game plan.

But even they were at odds with the loyalty he still felt toward a man who had taken him, wet behind the ears, and molded him into the successful man he was today.

Jared sighed. It was one hell of a mess.

Especially when he found himself desperately wanting to throw caution to the wind and tell Demi—no, *warn* Demi—about what Winfield was up to.

But even that route wasn't simple. He was part of Winfield, Inc. Part of the world she held suspect. If he told Demi about Winfield's game plan, she might think he was just trying to set her up. At this point, if he risked everything, his entire future, to tell her the truth, it would cut him to shreds if he saw distrust in her eyes.

He'd never been so damn confused before. Personally, professionally, in every damn sort of way, it felt as if his whole world had been upended.

Needing to regroup, he went home.

Theresa popped up like a jack-in-the-box set on a timer when he opened the front door. Her greeting was quick and sweet. Here, at least, he knew where he stood, Jared thought.

Theresa hung on to his arm, skipping beside him, obviously excited that he'd kept his word. He'd come home to take her to the restaurant, just as he'd done every day now for more than two weeks.

But her smile faded into a puzzled expression as she looked up at him, her small, sharp eyes studying his face. "You look sad, Daddy."

She was far too young to understand and far too innocent to be told that the world could be such an imperfect place at times. He ran his hand along her soft, silky hair.

"I'm fine, honey. I've just got a lot on my mind, that's all."

Theresa brightened, positive she had the perfect cure for whatever was wrong with her daddy. "Let's go to see Demi. She'll make you smile." She began to tug him toward the door again.

It was where he'd wanted to go all along. Not because it was his assignment, but because he just wanted to be there.

Just like the regulars who frequented Aphrodite, he realized.

He laughed at her eagerness. "You just want to go see Theo again."

She was too much like him to fib. "Yeah, that, too. Can we go, Daddy?" Her eyes were bright with anticipation. "Can we?"

It was a game, his pretending to resist and think it over while she persisted in asking. But today he really didn't feel like playing.

"Sure, why not?" One way or the other, he wouldn't be welcomed at the restaurant very soon. He might as well make the most of going there while he still could.

Lacing his hand with Theresa's, he called out to his housekeeper to let her know they were leaving and then walked out of the house.

There was no deluding herself anymore.

Demi knew the moment she saw Jared and Theresa walk through the entrance that she had been waiting for them to do exactly that all morning. Waiting and hoping, afraid that today would be the day that Jared would stop coming because he had found something better to do.

Or because he'd finally taken to heart her refusal to sell the restaurant.

That would mean that the only reason he'd been coming around was because of business. She'd believed that in the beginning, but now, for the most part, she'd talked herself out of it. Now, with her defenses almost completely lowered, she wanted to believe he was here because he wanted to be.

Because he felt the same strange, wicked chemistry between them that she did.

She prayed that it wasn't all in her head and that she was just being a fool. That would be a very cruel reality to make her peace with.

Demi glanced around. She was relieved that neither her mother nor the two waitresses, nor, thank goodness, her brother was in the dining area right now. There was no doubt in her mind that her expression when she saw Jared walk in gave her away no matter how hard she tried to keep a poker face in place.

She'd never been that good at poker, anyway.

Demi crossed to them before the door had a chance to close completely.

"Hello, Theresa." She bent down to receive the kiss she exacted as an entrance fee. Small, soft lips brushed lightly against her cheek. "Theo and Alex are waiting for you. Maybe you can actually get them to finish their game and start fresh again."

"I'll try," Theresa promised solemnly. In a blink, she was off to join her elderly playmates.

Demi watched her for a second, a yearning filling her that she wasn't ready to explore just yet.

She turned toward Jared. "You've got a terrific little girl there. She makes Theo feel like a kid again."

He fell into step beside her as she walked to the booth that had become his whenever he came here. He noticed she had a Reserved sign on it that she discreetly folded and tucked away behind the menus she was holding. It made him smile.

"It must be rough," she commented, "raising a daughter all by yourself."

Rough wasn't exactly the word he would have used. *Confusing* was more like it. There were times he felt like a man stuck in the middle of a maze.

Not unlike, he realized, the way he felt right now.

"It's getting easier." His mouth curved mockingly. "Or so I keep telling myself. Thank heavens her teen years are still far away."

"They'll come faster than you think. My mother claims I was a handful." Since business was still light, she took a seat beside him. She could easily see the front door from where she sat—if she didn't keep looking at his eyes.

A handful. He bet she was. "And the difference between then and now is—?"

She'd never liked being teased before. The warmth that traveled through her was something new. "Very funny. I'm much more subdued and conscientious now than I was then."

Jared didn't bother trying not to laugh. "More subdued? As compared to what? A rampaging panther? The Road Runner?"

She wasn't quite sure if she liked the images he was raising. She certainly had never seen herself that way. "Is that how you think of me?"

He looked at her for a long moment. "I try very hard not to think of you, Demi."

"Oh." She supposed she had that coming. That's what she got for letting herself daydream.

He raised her chin with the crook of his finger until their eyes met again. "Unfortunately, I'm not succeeding very well. Or maybe at all."

How did he make her understand without taking too great a risk himself? He'd been vulnerable once and had nothing but scars to show for it. No, he amended, that wasn't true. He had Theresa. The risk *had* been worth it.

Maybe it would be this time, too.

Her smile curled deep in her belly before it wound its way to her lips. "Oh."

He wanted to kiss the smile from her lips until he absorbed it all himself. "Yeah, 'oh.'"

Tucking his admission next to her heart, she looked at him more closely. He looked worn. Something was bothering him. "You look tired, Jared. Are you feeling all right?"

It looked as if he couldn't sneak anything by the women in his life, he mused. He gave her the same excuse he'd given Theresa. "Just got a lot on my mind."

Common sense told her to leave it alone, but she'd never strictly been ruled by brain cells. "Anything I can help with? Other than the obvious, which you already know the answer to."

That was as close as they had come to talking about the restaurant these last few days. And it was closer than he wanted to be right now. It was part of the problem. His problem, not hers.

Jared shook his head. "No, this is something I'm going to have to work out for myself."

Demi knew that whatever was bothering him involved her in one way or another. He didn't look as if he was up to a debate, and neither was she. For now, she left it alone. The only thing she could do was pass on the same bit of advice Theo had once given her.

She leaned in closer to Jared, so close that she could feel his breath on her cheek. So close that she desperately wanted to kiss him instead of talk. Had to be that hot Greek blood Theo was always promising her would someday erupt.

Talk about timing.

"Despite who you work for, you're a good man, Jared. Just follow your heart and your conscience and you can't go wrong."

She might think it was that easy, but he wasn't all that sure it was a safe bet. He might have a conscience, but it was beginning to look as if Winfield didn't. It wasn't an easy thing to remind himself that he was still collecting a paycheck from the company.

"What is it you have against Winfield, anyway?" The question was born of desperation. Maybe if he could turn her around, he could salvage all the pieces and no one would get hurt.

She didn't want to argue with him, but she would if he began to defend the man.

"I see him as this giant eating machine, swallowing up everything that gets in his way." Demi wanted Jared to understand her position. More than that, she wanted to win him over to it. "I don't care if Winfield owns a restaurant chain, but there should be room for the independent restaurant, too. Aphrodite is too different to be part of something else." Demi searched his face, looking for the honesty she'd come to expect from him. "You can't tell me if his brand was stamped on Aphrodite that he would run it the way my family has all these years."

"There'd be more of a profit." He knew he wasn't answering her question.

"Exactly." Demi paused. She didn't want him to think she was pontificating. There were very down-to-earth reasons for the way she felt. "Don't misunderstand—I think money is a wonderful thing, but it isn't a deity unto itself. Money is only as good as what it can accomplish. We own the restaurant, which should translate on some ledger to a nice amount of money. What we choose to do, what we've always chosen to do, is instead of pocketing that money, once in a while, if someone is hungry, we feed them. And when they have money, they'll pay."

He knew all about her generosity. Or her stupidity, as Winfield had put it. "Like that banquet you booked a month ago? The Ferregamoes?" he reminded her when she said nothing.

She looked at him sharply. She didn't like the idea of someone spying on her, going through her records. Even him. "How did you know about that?"

"Research," he answered mildly. "They gave you a down payment and then managed to get you to do the banquet on good faith."

Was that her imagination, or was he sneering at the term? Had she initially been right about him after all? Oh, God, she hoped not.

Demi dismissed the whole story with a wave of her hand. "It wasn't that big a deal and Ma went to school with Gina Ferregamoe's mother."

"Which doesn't entitle her to play on your sympathies."

Didn't he have a heart after all? "It was a wedding reception."

"Right. A wedding, not a charity benefit."

Though she hardly knew the people involved, she took umbrage on their behalf. Family celebrations were very, very important to her.

"It wasn't charity," she insisted. "They'll pay."

In his experience, people hardly ever lived up to the faith people placed in them. "Maybe."

Her eyes narrowed as indignation darkened them. "They'll pay."

The argument Jared felt they were on the cusp of was postponed only because Antoinette chose that moment to come looking for Demi.

Barely nodding at Jared, she turned immediately to Demi. "We have a problem. Mrs. Leyton says that they cannot send us the shipment of vegetables we ordered until they see some money."

Demi passed her hand over her forehead, feeling a

major headache coming on. "They get their check the first of the month, same as everyone."

Antoinette pressed her lips together. "You were short the last time," she reminded her.

"I explained all that to them." Things were tight right now. Mrs. Leyton had said she understood. Had even empathized, recalling her own early days when she and her husband had first gone into the supplier business. Demi rose. "I'll talk to her," she told her mother.

Jared followed in her wake. "How much do you need?" he asked.

Demi swung around. Oh, no, it wasn't going to be like that. "I don't need your money and I don't need to be in debt to your boss, either."

He tried not to take offense at her tone, and at the wary look that had come into her eyes. After three weeks, they were suddenly at square one again. "This would be strictly me."

That didn't change anything. "And the answer is strictly no. I was running Aphrodite before you waltzed in, Panetta, and I'll be running it when you waltz out again, so keep your checkbook in your pants." With that, she closed the office door on him.

Jared shoved his hands deep into his pockets. He felt as if he'd just been shut out of more than a crammed office.

"She does better alone."

He turned, startled. He'd forgotten Antoinette was behind him.

"Business-wise, she does better alone," she clarified. The last thing in the world she wanted was for this man to walk away from her daughter. "I know she won't tell you this, but she does appreciate the offer. Demetria is very stubborn."

"Really? I hadn't noticed."

Antoinette smiled at his comment. "She likes to do things her way or not at all. No one has ever taught her about the word *surrender*."

He didn't want Demi to surrender. That would change her and he liked her the way she was. But there had to be some give-and-take here. "How about compromise?"

Antoinette considered that for a moment. "You could try." Taking him by the hand, she led him to the worktable where she deftly picked up a serving of a custard-filled pastry, kataife, and placed it on a handy plate. She held it before him like a prize, one hand still on his wrist. "Come, why don't you try this? It's fresh. She may be in there a long time. Demetria does not stop talking until the other side says yes."

He had absolutely no trouble believing that.

Jared was just taking a second bite of a dessert that he thought in all honesty deserved the term "out of this world" when he saw Demi walking into the dining room. He stopped eating. She went straight to her mother. "We have vegetables."

Antoinette rose from her seat beside Jared. "How?"

Pleased with averting a disaster, Demi forgot that

she didn't want to talk about this in front of Jared. "I told Mrs. Leyton the full amount of the check would be on her desk tomorrow morning."

Antoinette's skepticism grew. "How?"

Demi shrugged, annoyed at having her back to the wall. "I have a little saved. Enough to cover that and to carry us for a while with the Leytons and the butcher." She saw the question in her mother's eyes. "Mr. Schmidt called, too. Seems everyone suddenly wants their money."

Antoinette didn't love the restaurant the way Demi did. Unlike Demi, she hadn't been born to it. Her first concern was her family and the toll this would take on her daughter. "Demetria, perhaps you had better listen to Jared and think about—"

Demi cut her short. "I'll listen to anything Jared has to say, as long as it doesn't have the words *Winfield* or *sell* in it."

He studied the dessert in front of him, a kernel of an idea forming in his mind. "How about the word *party?*"

They didn't have the banquet room booked this weekend. The extra money would be more than welcomed. "Now that I like."

"Okay." He looked up. "I'd like to have a party here."

She was instantly deflated. Didn't he get it yet? She didn't want to be in debt to him in any manner, shape or form, even if Winfield didn't figure into it, which she had more than a passing suspicion that he did. "I won't take charity."

Jared was starting to get annoyed. He was only trying to help her. "Oh, so it's okay to give it, but you won't accept it—is that it?"

She fisted her hands on her hips. "Jared, I already told you—"

He saw the distressed look on Antoinette's face and collected himself.

"Yes, you told me, but this is legitimate. You ask the little chess shark over there." He nodded toward his daughter. "She knows. I was going to have a party catered at my house this Saturday. I've decided to move it here."

She wasn't buying it. "And just when did you make this monumental decision?"

"Just now."

"Aha." It just proved her point. "Charity."

"No, kataife," he corrected, pushing the plate forward. "Your mother just served me something fresh out of the oven, which is the closest thing to heaven next to your lips I've ever sampled."

The comment brought a huge smile to Antoinette's face. "I will leave you two to your talking."

She moved away, doubting that either one of them even noticed. It didn't matter. Things appeared to be progressing just fine.

9

Demi waited until her mother was out of earshot. She didn't feel up to being attacked on two flanks at the same time.

Keeping her voice low, she said, "I told you, I don't want any favors from you. I'll find a way to pay everyone back—including the bank." She saw no point in pretending that he didn't know about the bank loan. He'd obviously made it his business to know about everything involving Aphrodite.

And he'd thought he'd won her over. He should have known better. When it came to being stubborn, this woman was in a class by herself.

"So you're turning my offer down?"

There was no denying that she needed the money. Badly. But there had to be another way to get it. She couldn't accept money from him. They'd never remain on equal footing if she did.

Demi squared her shoulders. "Yes."

She had a lovely neck, and right now he could just as easily envision his fingers wrapped around it as his lips pressed against it. Jared shook his head. "It's business sense like that that got you into this hole in the first place."

Criticism was not something she accepted kindly and now even less than usual. Just what was he up to?

"Why are you throwing business my way?" she demanded. A Hatfield didn't suddenly offer to help a McCoy. "For that matter, why are you giving me 'tips' on how I should run my business? Whose side are you on, anyway?"

The answer was simple, though ultimately it would cost him a great deal. "Yours."

What was it about the man's eyes that made her forget everything but the intense desire she'd tasted when he kissed her? Desire within him, within her.

"I wish I could believe that." She'd never meant anything more in her life.

He covered the clenched hands on the table, forming a silent covenant.

"Believe it." He paused, thinking. "Would you feel better if we compromised?"

And just what did that mean? "How?" she asked guardedly.

He tried not to let her tone bother him. Logically he could see why she'd still be wary. Emotionally he had trouble dealing with her distrust.

"I'll have the party at my house as originally planned." That way, he wouldn't be paying for the use of the banquet room. "But you'll cater it." He didn't put it in the form of a question. This time he wasn't about to take no for an answer. "Oh, and one more thing."

Here it came, the kicker. The payoff. She braced herself to be disappointed in him. "Yes?"

"You're invited."

There was no extraneous noise in the restaurant, just the gentle murmur of voices melding with the soft, piped-in music in the background. She couldn't blame it on that, yet she was still sure she hadn't heard him correctly.

"Excuse me?"

She looked adorable when she was confused, he thought. She'd probably rip his heart out if he said that out loud. She wasn't the type who appreciated being thought of as vulnerable.

But she was and it was that core of vulnerability in the midst of her strength that hooked him and reeled him in. Vulnerability needed to be protected. And he needed to be needed.

"I want you to attend the party." He said it slowly so that it could sink in. "There are some people coming whom I want you to meet."

One man in particular, Jared thought. A man who could do a lot for Demi if he liked her desserts half as much as Jared did. The idea had occurred to him just now, as he'd been sampling the kataife.

Demi bit her lower lip. Maybe she was being too stubborn about this. After all, it wasn't as if he were giving her a loan; this was strictly business. She brought the food and he paid for it. Simple.

As if anything involving this man could really be simple, she thought. Just being around him was complicated. He represented the enemy, yet she was so strongly attracted to him, she couldn't think straight.

"All right, I'll come to your party." A smile lifted the corners of her mouth slowly just before it slipped into her eyes. "You're just trying to get a good deal on this."

He breathed a silent sigh of relief. Getting her to agree had actually been easier than he'd anticipated. "I have a feeling I already am."

She tried not to let him unsettle her, but it wasn't easy. "What about Winfield—won't he object?" The man wouldn't take kindly to having Jared go out of his way for her. Especially since she had absolutely no intentions of capitulating.

He didn't want to spoil the moment by talking about Winfield. "You leave him to me."

"He won't be there, will he?" If he was, all bets were off. There was no way she was going to be put into a position where she was serving him.

Jared laughed. He thought she gave him more credit than that. "Do you really think I'm reckless enough to invite you to a party that he's attending?"

"No, I guess not." Demi put out her hand. "Okay, you have a deal." Warmth seeped through her as he shook it. Flushed, she withdrew her hand. "Now, just what kind of a menu did you have in mind?"

Though he liked everything he'd sampled at the restaurant, his interest was primarily centered on the baklava and the kataife. "The only thing I'm definitely sure of is that I want you to bring baklava. Lots of baklava. And kataife."

Cooking might be the way to a man's heart, but compliments on her cooking were definitely the way to hers. "That hooked on it, are you?"

"You have no idea." If he told her what he had in mind, she'd balk. If he knew her, and he was beginning to, she'd probably accuse him of trying to manipulate her life. The easiest way to do this was just to buy some and bring it to the man, but he wanted his friend to meet Demi. It seemed only fair.

"All right, baklava and kataife it is." She needed to start ordering extra ingredients. "How many people are invited?"

Jared did a quick tally. "Counting you and me, twelve."

A nice, small number. Piece of cake, she thought. Or, in this case, baklava. "All right, why don't I give you a menu and we'll see what we come up with?"

He already knew what he had come up with, he thought as he watched her walk to the hostess desk to get a menu for him. Trouble with a capital T. But he couldn't just stand by and watch her being squeezed out of business, which was exactly what Winfield intended to do.

It hadn't been his imagination; Winfield had changed in the last few years. The man he had come to work for *had* been an honorable one. Somewhere along the line, Jack Winfield's honor had gotten drained, sacrificed on the altar of a growing greed that demanded he forsake all his principles.

If he had had any doubts about Winfield before, the phone calls Demi had just gotten from her green grocer and her butcher eliminated them. Obviously tired of waiting for him to strike some sort of amicable deal, Winfield was going for the jugular. Jared wasn't about to allow him to do that. Especially not to Demi. He'd gotten too involved with her, with all of them. Theresa had gotten too involved. He couldn't bear the look he knew would be on his daughter's face if she should discover that he'd had a hand in helping Winfield make Demi sell her restaurant.

For whatever it was worth, he was going to throw in with the losing side, and maybe, by joining forces with it, he'd turn the tide. After all, armed with a paltry slingshot, some rocks and a great deal of determination, David had avoided being crushed by the powerful Goliath.

Maybe history could repeat itself.

Or, at the very least, Winfield would lose interest in acquiring the little restaurant and turn his sights on buying out another one.

Whatever the future held, Jared knew he had to take this step if he was ever going to look at himself in the mirror again.

Nerves, he thought, just nerves.

Jared tried to shake free of the uncomfortable feeling as he thought about the party that night. He wasn't accustomed to it. Since he'd become part of Winfield, Inc., he'd attended and given countless dinner parties for an entire spectrum of reasons. Along the way, he'd become an old hand at mingling, at subtly turning small talk toward the proper channels.

So far, he'd always had a fortuitous way of getting people to come around to his way of thinking.

Which was why Demi had been such an revitalizing challenge. One he'd decided to retreat from, not because he'd lost his touch, but because he'd begun to really understand what it meant to her to have Aphrodite. And what the place meant to others. Not financially but emotionally. You couldn't put a price on that, even though Winfield thought he could.

All those other parties he'd both attended and given had always revolved in some way around his work. But this time the purpose had changed. Rather than using it to promote and prematurely introduce Winfield's latest venture as he'd originally intended, this party was for and about Demi. That made it personal and raised the stakes considerably.

Since she wouldn't accept his financial help, this orchestration was the only thing he could do. There was a lot riding on tonight. The continuation of her restaurant for one.

The way she felt about him for another.

He tried not to dwell on that.

Demi arrived early to set up.

Armed with a host of pots and pans in various

sizes, she lay siege to the kitchen. Like a general establishing a beachhead in enemy territory, she deployed to their tasks the two women the temporary agency had sent her.

Even though everything looked as if it was going smoothly, she looked a little uneasy.

"Anything wrong?" Jared asked. He wasn't accustomed to seeing her with a dubious expression.

She shrugged off the question. "Catering in someone else's house isn't something I'm used to." Her own kitchen was better suited to keeping everything warm. For one thing, it was a lot larger. For another, she knew where everything was. This kitchen felt like a shiny, miniature mausoleum. "Maybe I should have had you come to the restaurant."

That would teach her to argue with him. "Too late now." Because no one was looking, he snuck in a quick kiss. He liked the quick flush of pleasure he saw on her cheeks before she caught herself. "Anything you want me to help with?"

He'd rattled her. She didn't like being rattled. Not when she was working. She needed a clear head.

Demi snorted at his question. "Yeah, like I'd let you handle the food. You just go and get ready." She began to usher him toward the hall. "We'll handle it from here."

He had a hunch she'd say that. "Don't forget, I want you at the party."

Demi nudged him on his way a little harder. "I didn't forget."

Jared hesitated, wondering if there was a proper way to phrase this. None that he could think of. He forged ahead anyway. Tonight was important and she needed to look her best.

His eyes swept over her. "Is that what you're going to be wearing?"

She looked down at the simple pullover and jeans she had on. "While we're setting up, yes." What did he think she was going to do, come dressed to the teeth and start stirring the avgolemono sauce?

He knew he was treading on dangerous ground, but it was a journey he had to take. "But you brought something to change into, right?"

"I'll be wearing the entrée, strategically placed." She pressed her lips together impatiently. "Yes, I brought something to change into." She'd even gone so far as to ask for Nancy's help. Between them, they'd located just the perfect dress. Or, at least, according to Nancy they had. "Now go. You're beginning to make me nervous."

He grinned, his eyes teasing her. "Well, it's about time."

Shaking her head, she waved him away. But she was smiling when she turned back to her work.

Jared was just slipping on his jacket when he heard the doorbell chime. Adjusting his cuffs, he hurried into the hall.

Out of habit, he glanced toward his daughter's room, even though she wasn't there. Theresa had been invited over for a pajama party at a friend's house. Everything was dovetailing nicely.

It just had to continue that way for a while longer.

His housekeeper was just closing the front door behind the first two people to arrive, Ted and Christine Wexler, when he reached the bottom of the stairs. Jared crossed to them, his hands outstretched. He wanted to get them alone before the others began arriving.

"Ted, Christine, you have no idea how glad I am that you could make it."

"Had to," Ted told him. "Christine loves your parties. She'd never forgive me if I'd made other plans for tonight."

"I always said you had taste," Jared told the older woman. Taking Christine's arm, he escorted her to the living room. Ted followed.

It was the first look Jared had at what Demi had done in preparation for the party. His wet bar had been extended, its supply supplemented with Aphrodite's own stock. Bottles, some colorful, some quaint, of Greek liquors were strategically placed to both convey the ethnic theme Jared was going for and catch the light. They glistened, inviting attention. There were small, covered tables set up here and there, bearing fruit and various selections of finger food, temptingly arranged.

From where he stood, Jared could see the dining room. The long, glass-topped table was elegantly set for dinner. But it was what was on the side that drew his attention—a slim table whose only function was to bear a large silver tray.

On the tray was a veritable mountain of baklava.

Jared lost no time in ushering his two guests toward it. "Ted, I'm going to do you a very big favor. I'm going to let you get to heaven without the daunting preliminary process of dying first."

Drawing closer to the side table, he saw that Demi had outdone herself. She'd brought not just one kind of baklava, but three. Almond, walnut and chocolate. He was tempted to indulge himself, but he couldn't eat and talk at the same time. There was business to see to first.

With small silver tongs, he picked up one of each kind and placed them on a plate for Christine, then duplicated a plate for Ted.

Making no attempt to disguise his enthusiasm, Jared handed the plate to Ted. "Tell me what you think."

"You're being very mysterious about this, Jared. I've had this stuff before." To humor him, Ted took a bite of the pastry. A look of surprise, then abject pleasure spread across his face. As if each bite had a secret to tell, he began to chew very slowly. "No, I was wrong. I *haven't* had this before. Not this quality." He looked in wonder at the remainder in his hand. "It's fantastic." The next moment, it was gone.

Jared let go of the breath he'd been holding. "My feeling exactly." Out of the corner of his eye, he saw that Christine was on her second piece, eating with gusto.

A light entered Ted's eyes. Jared knew exactly what he was thinking. Exactly what he'd hoped Ted would think. All that remained were the negotiations. And Demi's approval.

He wondered where she was. He hoped that she hadn't decided at the last minute not to attend and go home instead. She needed to be here for this. To feel as good about it as he did. After all, the credit all belonged to her.

"Why don't you just let that melt on your tongue for a while?" he suggested to Ted. There was no need to twist the other man's arm. "I have a little business proposition I want to run past you."

"For Winfield?" Ted's white eyebrows rose with his question. It was hard to talk when his mouth was in ecstasy.

"Not exactly. Hang on a minute, I have someone I want you to meet." He looked around, but Demi still wasn't down.

Excusing himself, Jared went over to one of the servers. "Where is she?"

Preoccupied with pouring out exact amounts of wine, the woman took a moment before looking up. "She went to change." Her expression brightened as she looked over his shoulder. "Oh, there she is."

He turned, struggling to curb his impatience. He wanted to introduce her to Ted and get the ball in play.

His impatience vanished as the sight of her registered with his brain.

"Demi?" he whispered uncertainly.

"You sound as if you're not sure it's me." There was only one other couple in the room and they were very formally dressed. As was Jared. She hadn't fully appreciated, until this moment, just how good-looking he was. How was it that this man was still unattached? "You did say this was black tie, didn't you?"

"Yes, but..."

There was no but, and he had no idea why the word had even slipped out of his mouth. For that matter, he had no clue how it had even managed to get past his thickened tongue to begin with.

She took his breath away. Taking her hand, Jared drew her closer. The fragrance she was wearing was making him light-headed. "You're gorgeous."

Up until this moment, she'd been a little uncertain about what his reaction would be. She knew she would have been bitterly disappointed if he'd taken all her efforts in stride.

The look in his eyes made her feel beautiful. All the fussing had been worth it.

Courtesy of her sister-in-law's insistence, she had on a simple, floor-length black gown that hugged every curve like an amorous lover. It was cut in a deep V in front and an even deeper V that went down to her waist in back. She'd taken great pains to do her hair the way Nancy had shown her. It was in an upsweep with just enough tendrils cascading down her neck and temples to give her a slightly breathless appearance.

"You can close your mouth now," she whispered. She was very, very pleased with the look on his face.

He couldn't get enough of her. "Why didn't you tell me you could look like that?"

Her amusement grew. "What difference would that have made?"

"For one, my heart wouldn't have stopped beating when it saw you."

She tried not to sigh too loudly. "Sometimes, Panetta, you say the loveliest things."

He knew he was standing there gawking at her like some tongue-tied adolescent. With effort, he reminded himself that he had business to tend to. Her business.

"There's someone else here who has something lovely to say to you." Turning, he tucked her arm through his and led her into the living room.

Demi felt out of her element. She was far from accustomed to houses as fine as his, or to a guest list with people who regularly found their names in both the business and the social sections of the newspaper. "Why are you being so mysterious?"

He wished there was no party right now, that he could tell his guests he'd made a mistake and invited them for the wrong night. Alone, he'd be free to do what he ached to do. Lose himself in her eyes, in her softness.

The only consolation was the fact that she would

appreciate this, and him perhaps, if everything went right. "A little mystery brings excitement to the relationship."

As if they needed that, after practically setting fire to the office the first time their lips met. "I think ours has just about all the excitement in it that it can handle."

"Then you don't want to hear about the idea I have to market your pastries?" The question was asked so innocently, it took her a moment to absorb it. By then, he was pretending to walk away.

She grabbed for his arm, forgetting there were witnesses. "No, wait, what did you say?"

"I thought so." He grinned. "C'mon, there's someone here who wants to meet you."

He brought her over to Ted Wexler and his wife and made the introductions, then let nature take its course.

Wexler, the president of a growing chain of supermarkets, was always on the lookout for ways to stay one jump ahead of the competition. Two if he could manage it. Jared knew he'd be interested in Demi's pastries. It was a marriage made in heaven.

Demi listened to the accolades the older man heaped on her baklava, and then to the business proposition. She thought she was dreaming. It didn't seem possible. "You want to mass-market them?"

On his fifth or sixth piece—he'd stopped counting—Wexler nodded. "That's the general idea. You know, like that cookie woman, except these are far more unique than chocolate-chip cookies." He cavalierly shrugged off what had, until this evening, been an ever-present thorn in his side. "Everyone's got a recipe for those."

Caution prevented her from running with this. "You're not asking to buy the recipe, are you?"

"No, as I understand it, it's a family secret." He looked to Jared, who had quickly filled him in on the particulars when it came to negotiating with Demi. Unlike Winfield, Wexler was extremely sensitive to other people's moods and feelings. "We can use that, build on it. The public will love it. 'Come shop at Valley's, the supermarket that makes you feel as if you never left home.'" He held up his half-eaten piece. "This is home baking made easy for them. All they have to do is bring their appetites."

"And their wallets," Jared put in.

"Shoplifting is frowned on," Ted countered. He was feeling very generous right now. "Although I have to say that I would have risked it as a kid if I couldn't have afforded to buy something like this. They're wonderful." He popped the last bit into his mouth, then dusted off his hands gingerly. "Young lady, we are going to make a fortune on these. When do you want to start?"

She blinked, unable to process all this. It was too good to be true. "Wait, this is going too fast."

"Too fast? For you, Demi?" Jared said. One dark eyebrow arched in surprise. "I didn't think that was possible."

Even before she let herself daydream, she had to get some of the ground rules down. "You're not going to make me scrimp on these, are you?" she asked Ted. "You know, substitute different ingredients to save a few cents."

Ted looked appalled at the thought. "I want these exactly the way they are. Heavenly. We'll sell them a piece at a time, or boxed at a slight discount. I'm never wrong when I feel strongly about something. And I feel very strongly about this. You are going to be a very wealthy young lady, Ms. Tripopulous."

"Demi, please," she corrected.

This was why Jared had invited her—to get her together with this man. She wished he would have told her, but then, she might have been too nervous or too stubborn to come.

It occurred to her that he was getting to know her better than she knew herself.

"Let me talk to my partner for a moment." Excusing herself, she tugged on Jared's arm, drawing him over to the side.

"Partner?" Jared echoed. When had that happened?

She'd made up her mind and wasn't about to let him argue his way out of it. "Well, if this is going to be as big as he thinks, I'm going to need someone to handle the business end of it. As you so astutely pointed out, I'm not very good when it comes to business. I need someone looking out for my interests. Besides, I still have a restaurant to run."

He smiled. One that she could run, once this got going. "I know."

"So will you?" She searched his face for an answer. "Or is there some sort of conflict of interest with Winfield if you take this on?"

"No, no conflict." Winfield wasn't going to figure into the equation much longer, anyway. "Okay, you have a deal. We'll iron out the details later."

He waited for her to protest. She always wanted to know what was going on immediately.

But she surprised him by agreeing. "What?" she asked when he stared at her.

"Nothing, I just never heard you agree so easily before. You are full of surprises."

"Good, I wouldn't want to lose my aura of mystery, either." She winked at him and he had the strongest urge to take her into his arms and kiss her.

But the doorbell was ringing again and more of his guests were arriving. Whatever he was feeling was going to have to be put on hold a little longer.

10

Demi was standing in Jared's living room, looking the area over to make sure nothing had been left behind. Within her, an incredible feeling of contentment mingled with euphoria.

It had been one hell of an exciting evening, she mused.

She didn't even hear him when he entered.

Jared came up behind her and wrapped his arms around Demi, drawing her close to him. For a second, he just inhaled the fragrance in her hair and let himself relax. The last guest had been escorted out; the two women Demi had brought with her had long since left after helping her wash and load up the pots and pans.

They were alone and he was savoring the feeling.

The tender, fleeting kiss on her cheek undid her almost as much as the passionate ones they'd shared. She could feel her whole body tingling, reacting to the heat of his as it slowly penetrated.

Maybe it was wrong, maybe it wasn't going to go

any further than it had, but just for now she let herself enjoy the moment.

Leaning back against him, she absorbed every nuance, every hard ridge. His breath made the tendrils at her neck flutter. She could swear goose bumps were forming.

"You seem pretty pleased with yourself," she murmured, content just to stay here like this until time faded into nothingness.

Bending over, he touched his cheek to hers and was amazed at how comforting that felt. How good just being with her like this felt to him. "Shouldn't I be?"

Demi smiled to herself. Everything had turned out far better than she could have hoped. "It was a success, wasn't it?"

How he wanted her. Wanted her so much, he felt almost reckless. "In every sense of the word."

She turned around slowly to face him, very aware that her body was brushing against his. It was a struggle not to let what she was feeling ignite and take over.

"What made you do that? Bring me together with Mr. Wexler?" It was a completely selfless act, one that, if asked only a couple of weeks ago, she would have said he wasn't capable of. And yet he'd done it for her. "You know if this deal goes through, there is no way I'll sell Aphrodite to Winfield. I won't need to even consider it as a last resort." She couldn't begin to describe her sense of relief, but it was mixed with confusion. Why *had* he been so nice to her?

Tired, Jared drew her over to the sofa and sat down. Demi sat down beside him.

"There's no 'if' about it. I know Ted. Unlike some people," he said, thinking of Winfield with a twinge of regret, "he's still as good as his word. And yes, I know you won't sell. But I knew that before tonight. You'd go down fighting. And just before the final reel, all those people you and your family carried off and on over all the years would come marching in with their nickels and dimes and quarters, throwing them into a giant collection pot until the note was met."

Her eyes crinkled. "I think I saw that in a movie once."

Watching *It's a Wonderful Life* had been a Christmas tradition in his family. He'd never fully appreciated that tradition until he had a child of his own. Now he continued it for Theresa. Watching the movie with her gave him a thread of continuity he realized now he sorely needed.

Just as he needed Demi.

He slipped his arm around her shoulders. When she leaned her head against him, it seemed only natural.

"So did I. But until I met you, I figured it was just pure Hollywood fiction, aimed at the wistful side of all of us." He looked into her face—her lovely, exotically sweet face. "I didn't believe people like you existed."

"People like me," she repeated, her tongue still in her cheek. "You mean stubborn, right?"

He'd be lying if he said she wasn't. They both knew she was as steadfast as a rock.

"Among other things," he allowed. Jared began to play with the tendril at her neck, winding it around his finger. "I think your stubbornness is part of what helps you hang on and do those impossible things you do."

She felt his fingertips brush along her skin. Her breath began to grow short. "Like?"

Jared did a short inventory for her benefit. "Make incredible baklava in an incredibly short amount of time. Keep the restaurant running on a song." He smiled as he saw her eyes flutter. The excitement he sensed growing within her fed his own. "Convert people like me into true believers."

Her voice was low, husky. "And what is it that you believe in now?"

"Goodness." His eyes caressed her. "You."

She felt as if she was being seduced. Demi had no strength to fight it, even if she wanted to. And she didn't. "I like the sound of that."

He pressed a kiss to one bare shoulder. "Stay the night, Demi."

Everything within her yearned to be with him. Just a man and a woman alone together, nothing more. But there was more. There were other things to consider beside her own desires.

"What about Theresa? I don't want to take a chance on her seeing me waltz out of your room in the middle of the night to go to the bathroom."

Always putting others first. It was why he was so crazy about her.

"I have my own bathroom," he teased. Leaning into her, he kissed her neck, first one side, then the other. He could feel her pulse jumping beneath his lips. "And the only way she'd see you is if she was sleepwalking all the way from Lisa's house."

It was difficult to remain coherent with all this heat going on around her. "Lisa?"

"Her friend." He straightened to look at her. "She's at a sleepover."

"No" was getting harder and harder for Demi to say. "And your housekeeper?"

"Has gone home." He nestled her against him, nibbling on her ear. His tongue teased her, outlining the rim. "It's just you, me and the leftovers."

Glancing at her, he saw the war going on in her eyes. Demi's look—and what he assumed it meant—hurt him. Jared released her. "What is it? You still don't trust me? Do you think this is some alternate plan to get you to give in?"

She twisted so that she could face him. "That would mean I didn't believe you were attracted to me. And I do." She cupped his cheek with her hand. "You couldn't have kissed me the way you did, or been as gentle as you were just now, if you weren't."

He turned her palm and softly touched it with his lips. Her sigh shivered through him. "I could be the world's greatest actor."

Though it was hard, she pulled her hand away. She

didn't understand him. "Why are you doing this? Playing devil's advocate like this?" She had to know. It just didn't make sense to her.

The teasing, playful look left his eyes. What remained was quietly sober.

"Maybe because I want you to be sure, Demi. Very, very sure about us. I don't want doubts ruining something that has the potential to be wonderful." That would be worse than anything he could imagine—to have her and then lose her because she thought he'd deceived her somehow.

But Demi had heard only one thing. Her breath stood still in her lungs as she asked, "Is there an 'us'?"

He thought she was more intuitive than that. "Don't you know?"

"I think I do." She had her answer. Smiling into his eyes, she slipped her arms around Jared's neck. "I also think you talk too much."

He grinned in response, arms tightening around her. "It's the salesman in me."

Ever so lightly, she grazed his mouth with her own. She was ready, she thought. More than ready to give this man everything. He already had her love. He'd had it ever since that day she saw him holding her niece in his arms. "There's such a thing as letting the product speak for itself."

His mouth covered hers then, claiming what she offered over and over again as his heart beat wildly, calling to hers. Jared felt her body melting against his.

Desire soared as his blood began to rush.

Barely drawing in any air, he moved his head back to look at her.

"Oh," he said, as if the thought had just struck him. As if it hadn't been on his mind all evening. Perhaps even all along. "One more thing."

Anticipation was drumming heavily coated nails all through her body. She wanted to make love with him, not talk. "What's that?"

Framing her face with his hands, he memorized her features a second before he asked, "Demi, will you marry me?"

She was completely speechless for exactly half a heartbeat.

"What?" The question squeaked out of her.

"Will you marry me?" he repeated. Nerves began reconstructing their former habitat. What if she turned him down? Trying to shield himself, he strove for humor and lightness. It was the only graceful way out if she said no. "I've always wanted to marry a rich woman, and this would satisfy a childhood fantasy of mine. Besides, I am going to be unemployed for a while and I thought that maybe Theresa and I might need a free meal or two. It would be nice to have somewhere to get it."

There was a buzzing noise in her head as she tried to make sense out of what was happening. He couldn't be serious.

Could he?

Without warning?

When he moved to kiss her again, she wedged both hands up against his chest. "Whoa, back up and let me catch my breath." She had a feeling an entire oxygen tank wouldn't help. "Now, what are you telling me?"

His expression was mild. He did not look like a man who had just proposed, Demi thought. Just what was going on here?

"Which part?"

Was he doing this on purpose? She wasn't sure anymore. "Start at the end and work backward."

"Unemployed?" he guessed.

She nodded. It was as good a place as any to begin. "Why are you going to be unemployed?"

He laughed softly to himself. That part was easy to predict. "I don't think Winfield is going to oppose my letter of resignation, not after he hears what I've done."

This was all news to her. "When are you going to resign?"

"Technically, I already did." He tried to read beyond her surprised expression and couldn't. "I faxed him a letter tonight after Ted made you that offer."

She vaguely remembered Jared had excused himself and left her with Ted, his wife and another man named Hanley, who was a local distributor. She didn't see him for a while after that. But everything was happening so fast, her head felt as if it were spinning.

So that was what he'd been doing. Resigning. He'd helped her, knowing this would be the outcome. What could you do with a man like that, except love him?

"But you're still not unemployed. You're handling the business end of this venture for me, don't you remember?" Or had he changed his mind about that?

He'd thought that perhaps, when the deal had been offered, Demi had just said that because she was in a euphoric state of gratitude, and that once the dust settled, she'd rescind the offer, going back to handling everything on her own. Just as she'd always done.

"If that's the way you want it." Amid all the rhetoric, there was still only one question that mattered to him. "Does that mean you won't marry me?"

She didn't give him a straight answer. She was afraid to. "About that—why are you asking me?"

"I told you—"

She didn't want to hear stories or whimsical responses. This was too important to joke about. "The truth."

"Tough one," he quipped and then he nodded, conceding. "Okay. Why does a man usually ask a woman to marry him?"

Her heart lodged in her throat. "Because he loves her."

With a flourish, Jared pointed to her. "Bingo."

Demi shoved his finger aside. "I don't want to play bingo—"

"No?" Jared pretended to leer. "How about doctor?"

He was impossible. "Jared, you haven't even told me you loved me."

Now there she was wrong, he thought. "Yes, I did."

She was far from deaf, and a woman always remembered exactly when she heard those three magic words for the first time in her life. They hadn't made an appearance in hers. "When?"

Jared enumerated the instances. A man of action, he believed in deeds, not words. "When I faxed my letter of resignation. When I got you to cater the party and meet Ted. When I stopped trying to convince you to sell." Those were all ways of telling her he loved her.

It was true that he'd stopped talking to her about selling the restaurant, but she'd been certain at the time that he'd just switched approaches.

"You stopped being direct, but you were still after me to sell."

He had to be honest. Then maybe he'd win. "In the beginning, yes. I thought I'd keep coming around until you got used to the sight of me. Got to like me enough to trust me and heard me out without prejudice." He lifted his shoulders, letting them drop again. "I guess somewhere along the line, I forgot I was pretending and started believing in my own game."

A smile bloomed on her lips. "You really do want that baklava recipe, don't you?"

He took his cue from her tone. "Hey, if I have to

sleep with the head honcho." He ran the tip of his finger along her lips and enjoyed the way she shivered. It went right through him. "It's a sacrifice I'm prepared to make."

"You still haven't told me..." She wasn't going to beg to hear the words. But until she did, she couldn't accept. "Things."

"What things? That I love you?" He shook his head. "Hell, I thought that would be self-evident by now. Maybe I didn't realize it was happening while it was happening, but that didn't stop it *from* happening."

His tongue was getting twisted again. The only way to make her understand was to bare his soul. It took Jared a moment to work up the courage.

"I was in love once and I swore I'd never give another woman that kind of power over me. Where it would feel as if my heart had been ripped out and thrown through a plate-glass window if she left. But I never counted on meeting someone like you. Someone who reminded me about all the things I'd gotten away from. Treating people as if they were people and not just extensions of business propositions. Having time for my daughter, no matter how hectic the day was. Finding the time to kibitz at a never-ending chess game. Smelling the flowers." He smiled at her. "That's the part I liked best. Do you know your hair smells like flowers?"

She liked that, liked hearing him say sweet things to her. "And the rest of me?"

"Like baklava." The answer required no thought at all on his part. "And I have developed such a sweet tooth for baklava."

"Never mind the snow job." He was just trying to get her mind off what she'd asked him to say in the first place. "If you want an answer, you're going to have to say it."

"Say what?" he asked innocently. And when she punched him, he could only laugh. "Oh, you mean 'I love you'?"

Demi refused to give him the satisfaction of playing along. Instead, she just looked up at the ceiling as if she hadn't heard a single word.

The next second, he was pulling her down onto the sofa. Demi found herself pinned beneath him. His eyes were laughing at her.

She squirmed and only belatedly realized that she was just adding to the problem. "What are you doing?"

He laced his hands through hers, holding them over her head. It seemed safer that way. "Just making sure you don't laugh in my face and run off after I tell you."

She played it his way. "Tell me what?"

"I love you."

He said it so softly, she knew it wasn't an answer to her question. He was telling her what was in his heart.

"I love your stubbornness and the way that silly little chin of yours sticks out every time you think you're being challenged. I love the way you look with flour on your cheeks and dabs of honey on your fingers that I can lick off." As if to illustrate, he brought her hand to his lips and then slowly, one by one, drew each of her fingers into his mouth, suckling gently.

Demi squirmed again, unable to help herself.

"I love the way your eyes begin to drift shut when you respond to me. I love the fact that you care about people even if it's not practical or expedient. I love you," he repeated with feeling. When she said nothing in reply, he looked at her. "Well?"

Suppressing a smile, she cocked her head. "Well, what?"

All right, he'd let her have her fun. "How do you feel about me?"

"You're okay," she tossed off indifferently.

He took his revenge by tickling her mercilessly. Demi wiggled and tried to get away, but couldn't. He was too strong for her to shrug off.

"Stop," she begged. "All right, all right, I give in. You're better than okay." The laughter left, and a sweetness took its place. A sweetness ushered in by a feeling of utter contentment. "Better than I could have possibly ever hoped for. I love you, Jared."

That was more like it. "I can live with that." He shifted his weight so that his body no longer pinned her down. Jared looked into her face, into her eyes, searching for something that would give him his answer. "So, what do you say? Will you marry me, Demi?"

It wasn't a dream. He was asking her, really asking her. "You know, Panetta, I have to hand it to you. You finally came through with an offer I can't refuse."

He grinned. "It's about time."

"Yes," she agreed, bringing his mouth down to hers. "It is."

Epilogue

Jared wasn't quite sure if it was the anisette or love that was responsible for this exuberant, heady feeling rushing through his veins.

Probably a little bit of both, he decided as he looked around the crowded restaurant. The sign on the door outside said Closed For Private Celebration.

It didn't look very private on this side of the door, he mused with a grin. The music from the band swelled as he danced with the most beautiful woman in the room. The woman he had, just one short hour ago, promised to love and cherish until his dying breath. And beyond that if he could manage it.

Jared inclined his head, bringing his mouth next to Demi's ear. "You really know all these people?"

Out of the corner of his eye he saw Theresa dancing with her new great-grandfather. His daughter looked as if she were in seventh heaven. *Join the club, honey.* Theo showed absolutely no signs of being tired, though this was their third dance. There were some amazing genes in this family.

"Every last one," Demi assured him. From where

she was, she could see her mother beaming at her. Antoinette's feeling of triumph mingled with a touch of relief radiated clear across the room. "Except for your friends," she admitted, "and I intend to get to know them before the night is out."

He laughed and shook his head. "If I return the favor, we'll have to wait until the year is out."

Her eyes glinted wickedly. "I don't think I can wait that long."

Jared laughed, pulling her closer. "I love it when you talk dirty."

The clinking sound of a knife rhythmically striking the side of a glass penetrated above the music. Someone else wanted to see them kiss, a task that Jared thought he was bearing up to manfully, though he had lost count by the eleventh time.

He looked around, but the source of the sound was lost to him. "Are there a lot of voyeurs in your circle of friends?"

She tried to look perfectly serious. "Just the usual amount."

He wasn't sure if she was putting him on. "Do you think they're trying for some kind of record?"

"Everyone should have a goal in life." She grinned just before he kissed her.

Never, she thought. She was never going to get so used to his kiss that she could take it for granted. He was always going to make her head spin, her blood rush.

Demi savored the flavor of his lips a second before saying, "You know what's great about all this?"

You, he thought. "What?"

Her brother caught her eye. Guy winked at her, obviously pleased that she'd found someone to make her life as happy as Nancy made his. Married, she was married, Demi thought. Wow. She took a long breath, as if drawing the atmosphere deep into her lungs. "Everything."

Jared couldn't argue with that. He just had something to add. "I was going to answer that it's the beginning of a wonderful life together."

She smiled into his eyes, so content she thought she could hardly stand it. "Yes, there's that, too."

The clinking, sharp and urgent, began again. When she looked around to see who was responsible this time, she saw that it was Theo. He'd interrupted his dance to take his turn at the ritual. *Bless him.* "Looks like Theo has a request of his new grandson."

Looking over toward the man, Jared saw Theo silently urging him on with very expressive hand gestures. He *knew* he'd always liked that old man. "Can't disappoint the head of the family."

She nodded solemnly, offering her mouth up to his. "Wouldn't be right."

And, Jared thought, his lips meeting hers, he always made a point of doing what was right whenever possible.

* * * * *

BESTSELLING AUTHORS IN THE SPOTLIGHT

WE'RE SHINING THE SPOTLIGHT ON SIX OF OUR STARS!

Harlequin and Silhouette have selected stories from several of their bestselling authors to give you six sensational reads. These star-powered romances are bound to please!

THERE'S A PRICE TO PAY FOR STARDOM... AND IT'S LOW

$1.99 U.S. / $2.50 CAN. Special Offer

As a special offer, these six outstanding books are available from Harlequin and Silhouette for only $1.99 in the U.S. and $2.50 in Canada. Watch for these titles:

At the Midnight Hour—**Alicia Scott**
Joshua and the Cowgirl—**Sherryl Woods**
Another Whirlwind Courtship—**Barbara Boswell**
Madeleine's Cowboy—**Kristine Rolofson**
Her Sister's Baby—**Janice Kay Johnson**
One and One Makes Three—**Muriel Jensen**

Available in March 1998
at your favorite retail outlet.

PBAIS

Return to the Towers!

In March
New York Times bestselling author

NORA ROBERTS

brings us to the Calhouns' fabulous
Maine coast mansion and reveals the
tragic secrets hidden there for generations.

For all his degrees, Professor Max Quartermain has a lot to learn about love—and luscious Lilah Calhoun is just the woman to teach him. Ex-cop Holt Bradford is as prickly as a thornbush—until Suzanna Calhoun's special touch makes love blossom in his heart. And all of them are caught in the race to solve the generations-old mystery of a priceless lost necklace...and a timeless love.

Lilah and Suzanna
THE Calhoun Women

**A special 2-in-1 edition containing
FOR THE LOVE OF LILAH and
SUZANNA'S SURRENDER**

Available at your favorite retail outlet.

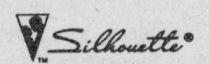

Silhouette®

Look us up on-line at: http://www.romance.net

CWVOL2

FIVE STARS MEAN SUCCESS

If you see the "5 Star Club" flash on a book, it means we're introducing you to one of our most STELLAR authors!

Every one of our Harlequin and Silhouette authors who has sold over 5 MILLION BOOKS has been selected for our "5 Star Club."

We've created the club so you won't miss any of our bestsellers. So, each month we'll be highlighting every original book within Harlequin and Silhouette written by our bestselling authors.

NOW THERE'S NO WAY ON EARTH OUR STARS WON'T BE SEEN!

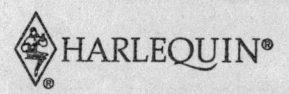

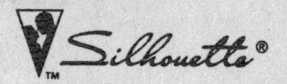

5 STAR CLUB AUTHOR

HARLEQUIN®   Silhouette®

P5STAR

SANDRA STEFFEN

**Continues the twelve-book series—
36 Hours—in February 1998
with Book Eight**

MARRIAGE BY CONTRACT

Nurse Bethany Kent could think of only one man who could make her dream come true: Dr. Tony Petrocelli, the man who had helped her save the life of the infant she desperately wanted to adopt. As husband and wife, they could provide the abandoned baby with a loving home. But could they provide each other with more than just a convenient marriage?

For Tony and Bethany and *all* the residents of Grand Springs, Colorado, the storm-induced blackout was just the beginning of 36 Hours that changed *everything!* You won't want to miss a single book.

Available at your favorite retail outlet.

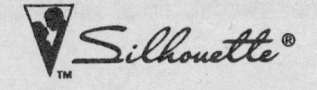

Silhouette®

Look us up on-line at: http://www.romance.net

SC36HRS8

SILHOUETTE YOURS TRULY™

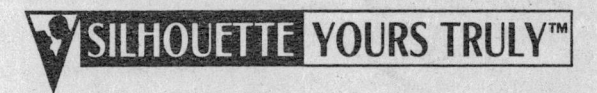

Sneak Previews of March titles from Yours Truly™:

WEDDING DAZE
Karen Templeton

Lost in a sea of silk, lace, something old and something new, Spencer Lockhart was definitely some*one* blue! This all-business baron of the boardroom hated weddings and everything to do with them. Everything except the gorgeous wedding consultant responsible for his sister's high-falutin event. It was a well-known fact that Brianna Fairchild could make anybody's wedding happen. Anybody's indeed! Spencer was quite sure she couldn't get him down the aisle…unless she promised to keep him company—*for as long as they both shall live!*

THE EMERGENCY STAND-BY DATE
Samantha Carter

Seems like nowadays a woman can't go anywhere without some gorgeous hunk in tow. And boy, did that have fiercely independent—and sadly single— Jenny Forrest up in arms. If only there was some way to appease the masses without compromising herself.

So she and her newfound friend, Ken Parks, agreed to be stand-by dating partners, the perfect solution. They had everyone convinced that they were a happy couple, everyone including the two people who were supposed to know better—themselves!

The Stars of Mithra

Three gems, three beauties, three passions... the adventure of a lifetime

SILHOUETTE·INTIMATE·MOMENTS®
brings you a thrilling new series by
New York Times bestselling author

Nora Roberts

Three mystical blue diamonds place three close friends in jeopardy...and lead them to romance.

In October
HIDDEN STAR (IM#811)
Bailey James can't remember a thing, but she knows she's in big trouble. And she desperately needs private investigator Cade Parris to help her live long enough to find out just what kind.

In December
CAPTIVE STAR (IM#823)
Cynical bounty hunter Jack Dakota and spitfire M. J. O'Leary are handcuffed together and on the run from a pair of hired killers. And Jack wants to know why—but M.J.'s not talking.

In February
SECRET STAR (IM#835)
Lieutenant Seth Buchanan's murder investigation takes a strange turn when Grace Fontaine turns up alive. But as the mystery unfolds, he soon discovers the notorious heiress is the biggest mystery of all.

Available at your favorite retail outlet.

Look us up on-line at: http://www.romance.net

MITHRA